of

SIX

A.K. KOONCE
ALEERA ANAYA CERES

MW00454581

Academy of Six

Copyright 2019 A.K. Koonce & Aleera Anaya Ceres

All Rights Reserved

Cover design by Killer Book Covers

No portion of this book may be reproduced in any form without express written permission from the author. Any unauthorized use of this material is prohibited.

This is a work of fiction. Names, characters, places, and incidents either are the products of the author's imagination or are used fictitiously. Any resemblance to actual persons, living or dead, businesses, companies, events, or locales is entirely coincidental.

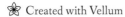 Created with Vellum

CONTENTS

ONE

Izara

Do you ever have harmless daydreams about ripping a misogynist jerk's dick off and shoving it down his throat until he can taste his own balls, just so he'll shut the fuck up for a little while?

Yeah. Me neither.

"It seems you've shown little to no abilities, transformations, or talents whatsoever, Miss Castillo," Headmaster Willms utters for the second time, flipping another cream page inside the folder titled: Izara Castillo, Age 19, Prodigium: Unknown.

The folder title alone is painfully accurate: *Prodigium Unknown.* What kind of supernatural am I? We have no damn idea. I'm basically a human in this man's eyes.

Except for the slip up that got me thrown under

Academy of Six's radar in the first place. Yes. I'm completely mundane except for that asshole my poor, innocent monster supposedly killed.

But that's something I don't talk about.

Partly because I don't remember it. And partly because it was my ex boyfriend, and when you kill an ex boyfriend, people start throwing brash words around like 'temperamental' and 'psychotic' and all that stuff.

Slaughter limb from limb one little ex, one time, and people treat you like you're dangerous or something.

"That's me. Little Miss Talentless. Are we done? Can I join the others?" I try to force the snapping words from my lips because it's easier than admitting how much this place is getting under my skin.

Flat black walls press in from the small space of his office. It dulls the shine of the old metal desk that separates me from the tired, old Headmaster. A little name plate sits at the edge of the desk with an excessive title listed there: *HEADMASTER DR. ALAN ABRAHAM WILLMS, MD.*

The Headmaster looks over his square rimmed glasses, his aging hazel eyes seemingly trying to search inside me with a single disturbing look.

"And you said you don't know what your Prodigium even is? A woman your age should know what lives inside her. Fae or siren would be my guess, judging by your alluring but cold exterior. But how do you live nineteen years without a hint of the Prodigium supernatural abilities showing? Is it a weak Prod or just simply ignorance, Miss Castillo?"

I give Dr. Willms another vacant stare and I almost stop myself from wondering if his dick's even large enough to fill his gaping mouth.

Almost.

"I appreciate the welcome into your prestigious Academy," *prison*, "but either assign me my classes to get my Prodigium under control, or let me leave because my shift at the Willy Hog Dog Shack starts in ten minutes and I'd really like to know just how terrible my future for the next two years is about to be."

Is it going to be customer-service-hot-dog-stink *average bad*, or like blow myself up during a strange Hogwarts style potions' class *extremely bad*?

Now we're both staring blankly at one another.

Finally.

He's speechless.

Until he isn't. "Ah, it seems they failed to inform you..."

Failed to inform me *what*?

This—this is why my father and I chose the human society of New York City. Humans, they tell you what they're thinking. All. Of. The. Time.

It's supernaturals who are conniving. Dangerous.

Deadly.

"Once you enroll at Academy of Six, we give you temporary restrictions. For safety reasons, I'm sure you understand, we do not allow students to leave campus, so

I'm afraid your work at the Willy Nilly... Shack... will come to a temporary end."

The smile against my lips is so repressed it hurts, but I keep it together long enough to hear a long and heavy sigh of apparent disappointment at my lack of reaction to skim from his lips.

"Take the standard schedule Mrs. Warren keeps at the front desk. We here at Academy of Six do not have the time nor the luxury to customize delinquent students' class schedules. Especially if they're not going to be around long." The pause he puts into this moment is so dramatic I wonder if he's theatrically trained or if he's just this good at being a total asshole. "You'll be in Dormitory J, fifth floor. Your schedule will have a room number randomly assigned to you. I wish you nothing but the best in revealing your Prod before it's too late, Miss Castillo."

Yeah. Thanks so much for that sincere welcome.

I shove out of the little wooden chair with so much force the legs scrape along the shining black tile floor.

I hope it scratches.

The cool glass of the door meets my palm and I push through it without looking back at the man who arrested me and also took me in. They're one and the same here at Academy of Six. This is the last stop for someone like me. Because there's a monster inside me. It either comes out and I learn to control it, showing the other supernaturals that it can play nice in society, or they'll throw my ass in confinement.

Innocent until proven guilty is a backwards statement in this place.

The door swings closed and the little woman typing away at her computer glances up with a hesitant smile just as she did when they hauled me in here. Her short curled hair is as dark as her eyes, and that half smile on her red lips is the same one you see in retail from cashiers who just know you're about to steal something.

I guess Mrs. Warren must be used to my type by now.

I grab the top paper she pushes towards the corner of her desk, but I don't pause to look at it until I'm out of the pristine faculty building and the afternoon sunlight hits my face. Warm air pulls at my inky hair and it finally feels like I can take a breath again. The walls aren't closing in on me. Men like Dr. Willms aren't lurking, waiting for me to screw up. *Again.*

I mean, he is. Just from a distance now.

I just have to be careful. I can be careful.

The tremble that shakes through my hands is so obvious that when I grip the paper harder, it doesn't even help.

I'm fine. I'm okay. Everything is going to be okay.

My lashes open slowly and I scan the thin paper, noting the scribbled number inked into the top right corner.

Room 503

FIRST YEAR PRODIGIUM

- •Introduction to Prodigiums 101
- •A History of Races
- •Demonology
- •Interdimensional Travels
- •Human-Prodigium Relations
- •Prodigium Health, *How to Care for Your Other Self*
- •Prod Reform
- •Gym

What the fuck! Gym? The Academy of Six welcome pamphlet didn't warn me that it was run by complete sadists.

Fucking gym.

If they tell me to run a mile here, I'll start at the starting line and not finish until I'm jogging through the doors of Willy Hog Dogs with open arms.

Wait, I can't.

Temporary restrictions. I glance down at the glowing gold band that now outlines my ankle, having appeared there as if by sparking magic. House arrest indeed.

This must be the only academy in the city that hands out class rings in the form of ankle bracelets.

Great.

I wonder if I'll implode on the spot if I cross the sharp iron, wrought iron fence that surrounds this "academy".

I'm still mentally pouting when I glance up at the

lush green grass and bristling trees. A dark memorial statue of an angel with wide spread wings is just in front of the entrance here. The script beneath her flowing gown reads: *Etheria, Founder of the Six, Former Headmistress of our hearts as well as our Academy. We are forever grateful.*

I narrow my eyes at the strange dedication and the Founding Angelic Headmistress it belongs to.

She stands tall like a goddess among us in the middle of the courtyard. Winding brick sidewalks circle around her, and building after towering gray building bleed shadows over the school yard.

Which one is Dormitory J? You'd think they'd have the letters displayed by the front doors. I guess they like to see us squirm.

"Lost?" A low masculine voice hums from over my shoulder. The sound of that single word lingers in my mind, my tongue flicking lightly to mimic the question, just to imagine the perfect way he said it.

When I turn, his demanding eyes don't match that perfection at all. Black, depthless pools create a void of color, filling his gaze completely with the startling gleam of his watchful eyes. But the sharp angles of his cheekbones, the strong line of his jaw, the dimple that kisses his cheek, it all diverts from how alluringly terrifying his eyes are.

I force my gaze away long enough to study his other features. His hair is white. Not the white of snow, not the sparkling crystals of frost sparkling like diamonds. This is no winter prince. No. His hair is the white of the sky. Like when the sun shines down from between pristine clouds in a blinding halo of light. That's what it looks like. A halo threading through the length of every strand.

How can someone who looks so angelically pretty have the pitch black eyes of a demon straight from hell?

"Uh..." I try to look away from him but it's hard. "Dormitory J."

He nods, a casual smile still clinging to his lips in the most distracting way. "Right. You're new too. Let me guess. Fae descent? High fae if I had to put money on it." His dark gaze drags slowly down my frame, starting at my inky hair and following the long length of my legs before coming back to my green eyes.

"You're the second person who's called me a fae today."

"They're delicate. Soft. Beautiful. A bit on the asshole side, but don't take it personally."

I can't help but smirk at him and his easy description that doesn't fit me at all.

Except for the asshole part. That's debatable.

"I'm not a fae. I don't think," I whisper with a lingering sigh.

He doesn't press me. Doesn't judge me like the Headmaster did.

But the silence that settles briefly between us makes me feel the difference between him and I. Between myself and every single one of these students.

They know who they are. Where they belong.

And I... don't have a clue where I came from.

When you're adopted, you always have little nagging questions in the back of your mind no matter how loved you are.

And when you're a mysterious Prod, it's even worse.

"Let me walk you. I'm headed to Juvie now." He walks away from me with confident strides. I barely have time to admire the black jeans hugging his taut ass like a second skin or the wide expanse of his strong shoulders before I'm rushing to catch up.

"Juvie?" I ask, a tad breathlessly.

His black eyes flicker to me but he doesn't break his stride. "It's what we call Dorm J."

"We?"

There he goes again, lifting those lips up into a dimpled smile. "You ask a lot of questions."

I usually don't, this place just offers more confusion than it does answers. For a school, they're not very good at educating.

"We Juvies, the poor Prod's who live there, and the Elites, I guess. If you make it through the first two semesters, *if*," he arches a sarcastic brow at that word but keeps going, "then you advance up into the better dorms. Dormitory E houses the second-year students. The real students basically."

If. That's all I can seem to think about. It's a taunting word that drills through my thoughts over and over again. It must be a big deal for them to put such an emphasis on passing year one.

"How many first years don't make it?"

He slows his pace and falls back to keep step with me, almost like he likes all my endless questions more than he's letting on.

"Statistically less than half make it. The ones who never find their magic, their *Prod*. Or, their Prod finds them and loses control. That is the real issue. They made Academy of Six to stop things like that from happening in society. So... just keep that monster inside you in check and you'll do fine." He winks at me, his severely pale hair nearly touching his depthless eyes.

"Yeah. Sounds easy. Release your beast, but don't release it too much. No problem." I push my hands into my leather jacket and he follows the motion, watching me out of the corner of his eye.

I don't even notice when we come to a stop on the far side of the campus. We're here it seems. I look up at the building he called Juvie. It feels a bit like Juvie. A dark shadow of color permanently stains the crumbling brick. The window on the lower level is boarded up with decaying planks of wood, and the shattered glass still lays in the grass like no one had the time to truly fix such a small imperfection on the already eyesore of a dorm.

The trees to my left are dry and decaying without any hint of leaves, their thin limbs wafting and ominous, really giving this place a homey vibe with every eerie rustle of their skeletal limbs.

I exhale slowly and follow after my new tour guide.

The very first step I take should tell me exactly how this year will go.

My white shoes barely touch the first step when the brick beneath gives away. A pathetic little scream crawls up my throat as I teeter backward the three inches off the ground I'd gained, hands flailing, my life flashing before my eyes, realizing it wasn't much of a life to really flash, more like a little flare than a full flash.

And then darkness falls across my face. Strong arms wrap around me, warmth searing into my skin from where his body presses into mine. Chest to chest, big dark eyes look down on me. And suddenly giant, heavenly wings spread out wide behind him, arching up from his back and making his shoulders seem wider, stronger now than they were before.

Droplets of blood coat the tips of the wings strangely. They glow, as if every feathery strand is laced through with the light of cold fire, casting his whole perfect body in an iridescent halo. The ethereal glow that surrounds him only serves to make those black eyes look more like shadowy pits filled with dark promises.

This man, this man is bad for me.

I know bad when it holds me in its arms and presses me all up against its delicious fucking body.

"Are you—are you an angel?" I stutter like a starstruck idiot.

The heat in his demonic eyes should answer my question.

"Do I look like an angel?" He rasps in the lowest whisper that fans across my neck.

Angels are rare. So rare most don't even believe in their existence.

This man makes me a believer. He looks like an angel.

He also looks like sex. That's what his Prod is. I'm convinced now that sex is a monster and this beautiful man is housing it.

I shake my head slowly. He's not an angel. Angels are innocent. Nothing in his dark, lust entrancing gaze is innocent.

"Come on." He steadies me on my feet, not explaining any more.

Maybe I've hit my limit on questions for the day.

With more care, I edge around the broken step, gathering my confidence and pretending like that flailing mess who nearly died on the welcome mat wasn't me. If they call this place Juvie, I need to never scream like that again in public.

I need to hide that fear deep down inside me.

I square my shoulders and keep going.

The walls are brick and the entrance has a nice little bullet proof glass window for someone to sit at, but the post is empty. My attention lingers on the dirty glass and the farther into the building we go the stranger the vibes get.

"The city donated this building when the Academy

first opened in the eighteen hundreds," my guide explains. *Vaguely.*

"What was it before?"

"A prison."

Wow. Dormitory Juvie just keeps getting better and better.

"The cells have been remodeled. Bricked over. They really wasted no expense as you can see."

"Clearly." I cringe when I leap over a dead rat in the middle of the black tile hall. I find a fearless pace again and pretend like I didn't just squirm because of a dead animal.

Fearless. I am fearless here.

The first friend I stumble upon in my new exciting life as a college woman, is a girl with long, white blonde hair. That's it. I can't make out her features because the man who's pressing her into the wall is... eating—kissing? —her face off. In his haste, his fingers fumble with the belt buckle between them and just before he pushes down his jeans I rush after my guide.

Hall sex? Seems kind of rude to do it in front of the innocent rat corpse. And gross.

A shiver shakes through my shoulders and I force myself not to glance back as growls and moans echo down the hall after us. Luckily, we start climbing a set of narrow stairs and it muffles their sounds, for the most part.

Sort of.

Higher and higher we climb.

When we come to a platform, a door with a square window to peek through is to our right, but we keep on trailing up the stair well.

"We're at the top. Late admissions get stuck on the fifth floor." He says it without glancing over his crisp white-gold wings.

The higher we climb, the hotter the air gets. It's so hot, that by the time we reach the door at the top of the stairs, I'm sweating. My long black hair sticks to the side of my face and I take small, secret gasps of air like I'm not ridiculously out of shape and completely pathetic.

Angel boy glances back at me, as perfect as if heaven just sent him down on a soft kiss.

The magical asshole.

He smirks at me before holding the door open, letting me pass and slowly trailing after me.

"Which room's yours?" he asks quietly.

I peer back at him and his attention is slow to pull from the low place he was just studying on my body.

"Were you just looking at my ass?"

There's that sinful smile again.

"Not at all."

Can angels lie? I wait for him to burst into flames for his sins but it never happens.

So either he's an honest man.

Or he's not a fucking angel.

Definitely that second one.

I glare at his crooked smile for several seconds before cutting my attention away from him. I don't answer him as I stalk away. When I reach 503, I turn the silver handle. The door opens with a burst of hot air that was pent up inside.

Before I slip in, his voice calls out to me.

"Not even a thank you?" His words whisper over the back of my neck and I find him right there, nearly touching me, but not.

He's fast. But what is he?

"Thank you," I clip out.

"What's your name, Prodless?"

Prodless. I have a Prod, thank you very much... I just don't know what the fuck it is yet.

"Izara Castillo, call me Izzy."

The inky depths of his eyes flare to life, like they hide fire somewhere in the darkest part of him.

"Iz-za-raah," he enunciates each syllable of my name like a purr. A deep, seductive sigh that I feel down to my toes.

My name. Has never. Sounded so. Sexy.

The pink of my tongue slides over my lips and he follows that move, his attention lingering on my mouth for so long that I can't even pull my own gaze away from him.

"Castillo," a deep rumbling voice says in perfect pronunciation. My name is spoken in slow, sexy flicks and rolls of his tongue. The sound of it circles my mind over and over again.

Everyone is really into my name right now and Juvie is finally looking like a place I want to be.

As for my jaw? It's on the floor. I don't need it. Talking's overrated anyway.

The one who spoke my name in a perfect Spanish accent leans shirtless on the far wall within the room, the open window blowing a slight cool breeze into his messy dark hair. Line after line carves his chest into a solid form of strength, his abdomen holding taut lines that ladder down to a deep vee at his hips. Eyes as warm as sunlight sink into me with that penetrating stare of his.

Holy sexy supernatural.

A comparison of Sam and Dean Winchester only flickers through my dirty mind for a single second.

Another man with dark hair lies on a top bunk against the wall on the right side of the room, his elbows holding him up as he stares down at me with the brightest blue eyes. His smile spreads slowly across his face like the devil gazing upon sin in the middle of a sermon.

It's unnerving.

And finally, my attention drifts to a man sitting on the bottom bunk on the opposite wall, his bare leg lifted, his arm slung over it in the most careless way. Fiery red hair hangs in his glaring green eyes. He's naked aside from a snug pair of black briefs.

Thank god for boxer briefs and the *massive* bulges they refuse to conceal. The gift that keeps on giving.

I still haven't spoken. I might not remember what words are at the moment.

Who needs words when three perfectly sculpted

men are staring at you like you're the person they've been waiting for their entire life?

"Shut the fucking door, you're letting all our cold air out," the hot ginger, with the apparently hot attitude, growls at me. Literally growls.

Maybe it's not me but someone else he's waiting on.

And then reality sinks back in to me.

"Wait," I call after my heavenly guide, turning to him because this is all a very obvious mistake.

"Syko. My name's Syko, in case you were dying to know."

I narrow my eyes on him.

"*Syko*?" I spit the word out. "Syko? I let some guy named Syko lead me into a dark condemned building and trusted him not to murder me."

"You trusted me with a lot more than that, let's be honest." I hate that smile on his lips right now.

"Syko," I curl my lips at that name. "Why are there three men in my dorm room?"

I'm not the type to complain when gifts are given, but this is clearly a mistake.

The carving smile on his lips lifts even higher, very devilish for a man who may or may not be heaven sent. He walks backward, letting the wide hall span between us before turning the handle to the door directly across from mine. "Overcrowding. They don't put a lot of effort into us first years. Half of us will be gone before the second semester even starts. You can change rooms then. Second years are more strict. Females in the left wing, males in the right. Until then, you tell me if any of your new friends fuck with you." Syko slices his attention to the men standing behind me.

Syko. I'm supposed to go running to a man named Syko if anyone scares me.

What the fuck is wrong with this place?

TWO

Phoenix

A girl. The random number game this shithole likes to play threw us in with a fucking girl.

Great.

As if the hipster wasn't bad enough. He fucking unloaded more herbs than an Olive Garden out of his duffle bag, decorating our room like a fucking greenhouse. And now, to top it off, the two of them are speaking quietly together in Spanish. As if by whispering, Saint and I won't know what the fuck they're saying.

News flash, I already don't know what the fuck you're saying and the conspiratorial tone it's said in just pisses me off even more.

My attention drifts to Saint and it's like the vampire knows exactly what I'm thinking just by looking at me. I hated that he could do that when we were younger and I hate it now. He reads people too easily.

It's fucking creepy.

And hot.

I shift my attention and pin my glare to the back of her inky hair. It curls down at the ends, wafting across the narrow span of her back, nearly touching the perfect curve of her ass.

She's wearing a leather jacket like she might catch a cold in this fresh hell they've tossed us all into.

The longer I stare at her though, the more I really notice her curves. The sliver of skin peeking out beneath her t-shirt and the way her torn jeans hug her body like a second skin.

The quietness of my chest gives an aching spasm, disrupting the emptiness just slightly. It's the smallest hint of emotion, a tease of feelings.

Then it's gone.

"Malek," Hipster says, his big hand sliding into hers with so slowly it's like he's fucking her palm with each roll of his wrist. *Jesus* just get out already. Go fuck in the hall like the rest of these people.

Maybe I'm bitter. I am. I know I am because Saint says I am. He's so good at reading people I don't even question it when he says something like that. I'd trust his word over a trained psychiatrist any day.

I'm tired of searching for real feelings though. It's an endless game that I always lose. I'm tired of being a fucking soulless incubus who can't feel sex. Sex, excitement, lust, any basic human emotions in general.

It's all bullshit.

I've tried. I've fucked my way through plenty of women and men, done the deed but never... felt it.

It doesn't matter. It doesn't define me.

That's what Saint says, so it must be true.

The humming sound of Malek's voice is this non-stop growl of flicking words and seductive tones.

If sex had a sound, it'd be that hipster asshole's theme song.

And I can't stand to listen to its tune any more.

I push off from the old mattress, ripping open the closet door and finding hanger after little wire hanger of khaki pants.

Fuck my life.

You know who wears khakis? People who can step foot in a fucking religious establishment without being burnt alive by holy water.

Not me.

I shake my head and tear the offensive clothing off its hanger. I pull on my assigned khaki pants like a good little academic student. I button the top button in silence. It's so quiet I can hear the *zzzppp* of the fly as I pull it up.

Why the hell is it so quiet in here? I can hear the silence of my fucking soul in this place.

When I turn, all three of them are staring at me.

"What?" My jaw clenches and I look back at the closet to find crisp white button downs mocking me.

Nope. Not doing it. I shouldn't have to wear a fucking tie.

"What?" I ask again, agitation clawing at my chest with each mute minute that slips by.

"Chick across the hall said you guys fucked," Saint says, amusement tinging his tone.

I search my mind, but I have no idea who 'chick across the hall' is. My shoulders lift. "So?"

Saint's lips do that slow slicing smile he gets when something really intrigues him.

"She said the soulless incubus had a tail. You know, little devil like tail? Spear shaped. Maybe red and swaying." He pauses, his blue eyes lighting up like fucking christmas morning over a goddamn tail. "Care to expand on that? I'd love to get the details."

A tail? What the fuck is wrong with people?

Somedays Saint is my best friend. But most days, he's a demented asshole.

"I don't have a tail. Sorry to ruin your fantasies, Saint."

"Really? Nothing? Not even a little nub?" His long tattooed fingers gesture, putting a small amount of space between his index finger and his thumb, gesturing sizes like the fictional nub might be growing with each passing second that I let his little mind run wild with disturbing—probably naked—images of my non-existent tail.

"Fuck, shut up. There's no tail. No...*nub*." My lip curls as I say that fucking word. The bastard just wanted me to say it, I think.

New girl keeps flitting her attention over every move

I make. Her watchful quietness sets me on edge. Like I'm being judged even if I'm not.

It's not her fault. It's my Prod's. It draws people to it. They crave the incubus's affection without even realizing it.

It gets me so much attention that I feel like I'm being crushed under it.

"What's your name?" The girl tilts her head at me, her body lingering close to Malek's like they're already an item.

An item I'll have to tolerate, watch, and listen to for the next four semesters.

I shake my head at both of them and, with too much strength rippling through my body, I pull the door open, letting it jar harshly against the frame before striding through it and slamming the heavy door shut behind me.

"Nice meeting you too, Nubbie," she calls after me, her smooth voice muffled but still ringing out with clarity.

My back stiffens and I realize I should have just fucking told her my name.

It's day one here and now my name is Nubbie now.

Fuck.

THREE

Izara

"He seems friendly." Not. And I'm going to have to put up with that asshole's attitude for the whole school year? *Just kill me now,* I silently beg the nameless, faceless Prod that lays dormant inside of me.

I search inside myself, mentally pulling and tugging, looking for any sign that the thing that murdered my ex is there.

I feel nothing.

I tear my gaze away from the door long enough to look back into the eyes of Malek to find his dark gaze already regarding me through the thick-framed glasses perched on his nose. The glasses look a bit out of place on such a beautiful face, but somehow add to the allure of dark skin and prominent features. His nose is relatively straight, his cheekbones high and flushed. The shadow of a beard peppers along his jaw, and when he smiles the gesture seems... *wolfish.*

"So what are you?" I ask, trying to appear casual as I make my way over to the bunk bed on the right side of the room. The bottom one is bare of covers, sheets, or pillows. Nothing but a thin, lumpy looking mattress with holes sheared through it to reveal uncomfortable metal springs beneath. I poke it with my finger and immediately feel like I need to shower.

Instantly, I take a step back and fold my arms over my chest, standing awkwardly but ensuring I won't have the urge to touch anything else for a while.

"Spanish," Malek replies, the grin that highlights his face bleeding into his sarcastic words, I whirl around to see the twitching of his lips.

I roll my eyes. "That was obvious from your accent. I meant what's your Prod?" *Is that a rude question to ask?* Whatever, I've been haunted with that question left and right from everyone ever since I got arrested. At least he can give me an answer that doesn't echo my own 'I don't know.'

Malek pushes himself away from the window and prowls towards me like some type of feline or predator, his dark eyes gleaming the color of molten honey in the light like I'm the prey he's cornered. I have this urge to step away, but my choices are minimal here. Step away and fall onto a disease-infested mattress, or stand my ground and face a man I don't know as he saunters dangerously close to me.

He seems nice enough, like someone I can be friends with, but I have to remember that every single person at this academy has a reckless Prod inside of them that has made them commit a crime. Just how dangerous are my new roommates?

And why the fuck do I feel a sliver of anticipation race down my spine instead of trepidation?

Maybe I'm just fucked in the head.

Probably. Possibly.

Another stalking step has another pulsing of my heartbeat thrumming between my thighs.

Definitely. Definitely fucked in the head.

Malek stops before me, far enough away to give me the illusion of space, but close enough that I can feel the heat radiating off of his golden kissed skin, see the very detailed ridge of muscle carved down his abdomen, see every droplet of sweat roll down his taut skin invitingly. Tattoos catch my eye. They trail up his arms in dark shadowy images I'm familiar with of Aztec warriors and conquistadors, sugar skulls, roman numerals, a moon, and a monster. Bits and pieces of his heritage are stamped on him like a badge of pride.

He has a body I itch to paint in smooth, even brush strokes.

Hell, he has a body I itch to lick in smooth, even strokes.

He bends a fraction so we're face to face, and whispers, his voice dripping like a dangerous promise of forever until the one word he says slashes through my senses, making me jerk back.

"*Licántropo.*"

Lycanthrope.

They threw me into a tiny cell of a room with a werewolf. My gaze goes warily to the man on the top bunk on the other side of the room, looming above us and watching the show. He's sprawled sideways lazily, his head propped on to his open palm as he takes in our interaction with mischief in his bright eyes.

I swallow, trying to appear the epitome of calm. They wouldn't hurt me. They can't. Not at the academy. Can they? I wonder just what type of restrictions the golden magical band around my ankle gives us all.

"And what are *you*?" I ask, relieved when my voice comes out steady. Confident. *Fake.*

In response, the man smiles and I'm gifted with the image of perfect white teeth, and the sliding points of incisors lengthening against his plump bottom lip.

"Jesus Christ," I mutter.

"No," he smirks. "I'm his counterpart, actually."

Fucking vampire.

Fucking school.

I'm an unknown Prod with no inkling or hint of power, trapped in a small raggedy dorm barely held together by fragile peeling walls and tape, with a werewolf, a vampire, and a fucking demon with a nub. Not to mention that asshole angel across the hall. Who knows what else lurks in this crumbling detention center of a place.

Werewolves, vampires, and everything in between thrown together. It all sounds like a deadly fight waiting to happen.

"We aren't going to hurt you," Malek promises softly. I can see his eyes soften into such tenderness, I'm already lost in the gentle depths of his gaze.

And then the vampire ruins it. *"Much."*

Malek rolls his eyes and turns away from me, making his way to the rickety closet. One closet filled with white shirts, khakis and four small drawers.

Are we meant to share that thing?

Swiftly he lowers his jeans. He takes out khaki pants and unfolds them.

He does it ceremoniously, as if it's the most natural thing in the world for him to dress in front of a girl he barely knows. And I can't help but stare as he bends over, his boxer briefs hugging his ass, as he steps one leg in and then the other. When he straightens, he reaches in again to pull out a collar shirt, a dark blue blazer, and a red tie.

My gaze is so mesmerized by those long fingers that I swear his mouth moves with what could be words.

Shit, he's definitely talking.

To me.

Focus.

"Did they give you your schedule?" he asks conversationally, though there's something suddenly stiff in his words, clipped and forced. The amiability is still there, but there's something different in the tone now.

"Yeah."

Fucking gym let's not forget.

He turns, flipping his collar and smoothing out his tie. "Classes are about to start. You should change into your uniform and head over to building A, that's where most first years take their courses."

I blink stupidly at the perfect picture this werewolf makes in his uniform. With those glasses and that build, he looks like he's meant for Harvard instead of Juvie. He's definitely distracting, but not enough that I lose myself behind those words.

I've barely settled in, it's my first fucking day and I'm expected to go to class? Where's the justice? It's like fucking military school.

"I don't have a uniform," I mutter. In fact, I don't have anything with me. The moment they arrested me, I was hauled from one barred prison cell to this one. I have no clothes, no shoes, no *panties,* and no paints.

Shit, my paints. A year's worth of money and pieces of art that I'll never get back are left forgotten in an apartment I'll surely lose by the end of the month.

"Here." Malek digs through the closet again and emerges with a bundle of clothes that he tosses my way. I catch them and watch the folds of clothes unroll to reveal a uniform similar to his. Prestigious academy blazer in dark blue, a small collar shirt and tie, except where he has khaki pants, I have a skirt.

I hold the items at arm's length. "It's kind of creepy that you just happen to have this in there." The uniform falls from my hands and onto the floor. While I was used to hand-me-downs, I'm not sure I trust the previous owner of this outfit to be disease free. Not with the way the students here obviously liked to hump in the hallways. *Ugh, I have two years of this to look forward to.*

My shift at Hog Dog's has never looked so appealing.

"It's new. The Academy delivered it the moment they brought you here."

Right. Magic. That's going to take some getting used to. While I'd been adopted by a warlock, he was excommunicated so magic had never been the norm in my youth. Even though I knew it existed, I never imagined I'd be sucked into all of this.

I thought I could live quietly just like my dad.

Academy of Six had other ideas.

My Prod had other ideas.

"Most of us never have time to pack our things," Malek explains. "Anyway, I'd hurry if I were you. Professors here are strict."

I can do nothing but watch helplessly as he grabs a backpack from the floor, hefting it over his strong shoulder. I feel suddenly empty, almost naked as he walks away. He's leaving me alone with a vampire, and I'm suddenly acting like a codependent dipshit. I straighten my shoulders and force my voice to come out steadily.

"Where's building A?"

Malek stops, throws a glance at me over his shoulder.

I can see the tilted smirk of his lips, wolfish and playful. "Saint can walk you." A moment later, he disappears from the room.

Slowly, robotically, I turn to the final male left in the room.

Tattoos accentuate just how pale his hard chest is, whisking lines that smoke down his arms and sneak up his neck. A single religious cross marks the space between his collar bones at the center of his throat, the tip of the ink reaching up to spear the underside of his jaw just lightly.

Saint. His name is Saint? What the fuck kind of vampire has the ironic ass name of 'Saint'? This one, apparently. And I don't particularly enjoy the way he stares at me. Like I'm a snack he means to devour.

Is he going to take a chomp out of me? He looks as if he's contemplating the thought, what with the perturbingly sensual way his tongue darts out across his lower lip and the way he won't stop staring...

Judging by the collectors assortment of crosses decorating his wall, I'd say those are not going to aid me.

All I have to protect myself is me and my quiet Prod.

So nothing. I have nothing.

Well, *fuck.*

FOUR

Saint

She's nervous. I can hear her heartbeat from here, the way it thumps like the trapped, frightened wings of a baby bird within a cage. Does she think I'm going to bite her?

How cute.

I'll let her believe what she wants, let her believe the worst of me because it's just too fucking fun to watch the way she squirms nervously in my presence. The poor thing has no idea that I'm not even the worst of the bunch. That honor goes to Phoenix.

A harmless vampire like me is the least of her concerns.

She stares a moment longer, as if by staring she can somehow predict just how dangerous I am to her, how out of control my Prod is. We're all new here, but she seems to be newer than most. Unseasoned. Like she's never grown up surrounded by the magically mythical and deadly dangerous. I wonder just how true that is. A dark part of me just can't help but want to test her. Push her.

Break her.

My eyes graze lazily up her figure, stopping at the pulse jumping at her delicate throat. Her long dark hair is in the way, some dark strands tucked tightly into the collar of her leather jacket, but I can still see the frantic beating of it.

It almost makes me wish I liked the taste of blood.

Her calm, controlled exterior doesn't match the drumming blood that's calling to me beneath her smooth untouched skin.

Not a scar on her. Beautiful, perfect, unmarked in every way.

I don't know why that's such a thrilling thing to think about.

"Class is about to start." I smile slowly and she stiffens at my words, glaring at the pointed look I give her uniform at her feet. "You should change so we make it there on time."

I should take my own advice, but I can't bring myself to care about anything: this academy, the classes... nothing matters. I was dumped here because no one wants to deal with me, but the teachers have to because my family funds this shitty place.

So I can arrive at whatever time I want, and anyone who has something to say about it can get fucked.

But pretty little Izzy, she should get changed, slide out of that jacket and glide that short khaki skirt right up those long legs, the soft curves of her thighs, up over her pus—

"What about you?" she interrupts the delicious trail of my thoughts.

Hmm, cute how she has a tiny dark freckle placed on her upper lip. She is rather pretty, the type of girl who doesn't quite realize how alluring she is. Who seduces without meaning to in the subtlest of gestures. In the way she bites her bottom lip, in the soft flicking of the dark strands of her hair. In the sassy cock of her hip. In the well placed position of that cute tiny freckle.

Cute. Pretty. Not sexy. She's attractive in a way you know she's delicate.

And this place. This place will fucking break her.

I smile in response and slowly unfurl my limbs from the bed, taking extra care to stretch and work out the kinks in my joints. I can feel the way she watches me as I hop from the top bunk and make my way over to our shared closet.

Tiny little thing on the outside, but blessed with witch magic to fit an endless amount of identical clothes. Because instead of investing time and magic in a dormitory that's *not* rat infested, they use it on stupid shit.

Like luxury closets.

It's nice to see that my parents' money is being used to its fullest.

I hook my fingers into the waistband of my boxers

and yank them down. A strangled gasp sounds behind me as I step out of them. When I stand up and turn, it's with a raised brow at the new roommate's blushing face and the way she tries so very hard not to look down at the jutting ridge of my erect cock.

It's a need, really. I physically need to make her uncomfortable just to see who she really is. Nothing tells you what someone is actually thinking like slapping your dick out on day one.

Gotta see how we measure up, if you get my drift.

"Is it necessary to flaunt your dick around?" She rolls her amber eyes and presses her fingers to her temple, covering her eyes out of pure annoyance. It doesn't matter one bit when she's peeking through the spaces between her fingers. She could get a better look if she just faced it head on. Literally. I'm right here.

"You make everything so much sweeter." I wink. "And in the spirit of fairness, you should probably undress as well. I showed you mine after all."

"Pervertido," she says in a flat irritated tone.

I don't speak a lick of Spanish, but I'm pretty sure she just called me a pervert. Never has an insult sounded so sexy.

What else can I get her to call me?

My cock twitches with a pulsing feeling at the thought of all the dirty names those lips could call me.

I feel the same way, I feel the same way.

I turn away from her cruel, sweet words. "Might as well get used to it." I reach for my own uniform to start pulling it on. "It's hot as hell in here all the time, and clothes are overrated. Are you dressed yet?" I can't keep the smile from pulling at my lips.

I can practically hear her growl at me. "Don't turn around! We share a room, not my body."

Yet.

She prohibited I look, so of course I casually do the opposite. Slowly, so I don't startle her, I turn and watch the swish of fabric fall as she bares herself to me.

Her body is all sinuous curves, slim waist and wide hips, a curved ass that presses tightly against black panties, partially hidden behind all that long hair. Holy Mother Mary, she's not wearing a bra, this fact made known as she flicks her hair over her shoulder to bare her unblemished, smooth back.

She's a temptress, and she captivates me entirely as she pulls the skirt up her long, gorgeous legs and shimmies into it. I never thought khaki could look so fucking sexy. On her it does. The hem of the skirt skims high on the backs of her thighs. If she bends over, I'll be able to catch another glimpse of black lace.

If she were bare underneath...

I swallow hard at the drilling possibilities filling my head.

Izara shoves her arms into her shirt, buttoning it up furiously. Next goes the blazer and when she turns, she's frazzled perfection.

Her lips blow long strands of stubborn hair away

from her face while she looks down and struggles with the tie.

The uniform is a fucking joke. They could have just as easily put us in orange jumpers like the humans do for criminals. That's what we are, after all. Criminals reforming. So wearing a uniform seems like some cosmic joke, some vicious form of torture.

Maybe it is.

The blazer has the academy's insignia stitched on the breast pocket; a shadowy number six in gilded gold and red. As if some old lady's cross stitch slapped onto a coat makes us something other than what we are.

Fucking criminals. Embarrassments to the supernatural society. A danger to others and ourselves.

Her slender fingers fumble once more and the way her full lips thin into a non—existent line tells me she's just about ready to rip the silk tie off and toss it to the ground.

"Here." I stalk forward, pulling the tie from her stubborn fingertips. She's reluctant to let it go, but a quick yank pries it from her grip. "No one's ever taught you how to tie a tie before?" My fingers brush aside her long hair. It's silk against my fingers, running down my skin like water sliding off of smooth stone. Light caresses brush across the nape of her neck. I feel her shiver, hear her heart speed up at the brief contact. Her blood rushes through her veins in a maelstrom. I can smell it.

Fuck.

I haven't drank real blood in three years—since high school—and all I want to do is find that spot along her inner thigh and sink my teeth into the soft skin of her body.

Let the warmth of her release fill my mouth...

Sharp teeth jut out, stealing space away within my mouth and I have to physically think about the most mundane things to get my fangs to go back to their normal length.

I never change my features, never give any sign of the danger she could be in if I keep thinking of her hot blood dripping down my lips, my fingers, my...

"Can't say that they have," she interrupts my thoughts my thoughts.

Her voice is a breathless rasp, and I feel the sound surge straight through to my cock, pressing uncomfortably against the zipper of the fucking khakis.

My fingers move quickly, tying the knot and setting it loosely against her chest.

And then too much space presses between us.

Again.

"Tighten it at your leisure," I lisp, aware that my incisors have come out to play again.

Having vampire teeth is like having a cock in my mouth—and not in a good way. They seem to have a mind of their own. Fuck, the damn things are so in tune with my dick that when I get hard, they make an appearance.

She flinches at the sight of them.

Instant incisor killer. My Prod is such a cock block sometimes.

I feel the sharpness slide back into my gums.

I smirk. "A piece of advice, Izzy: if you want to get through first year, don't flinch every time someone shows you the more primitive side of their Prods. It's a sign of weakness."

And she's going to need every ounce of strength she has to deal with this fuckery of a place.

FIVE

Izara

Building A is a luxury resort compared to our dorm. The graying brick crumbles into dust and debris in lonely piles on the ground. The windows are at least put together, and not one of them is boarded up.

That doesn't take away the ominous loom of it, though. Doesn't make it seem any more friendly. I doubt anything could do that. Even if they planted bright flowers in the dead, desolate gardens, it would look like nothing more than a mockery.

The place is literally devoid of color and happiness. At least on the outside.

When Saint guides me inside, the halls are boisterous with activity and life.

No hall sex, so I guess that's an improvement.

So many criminals in one place is bound to be trouble, and you can tell. Growls and snarls echo around the corridor. A couple of brown werewolves fight in a corner with teeth and claws. Flesh flies in bloody clumps, littering the white-tiled floors with the color crimson.

The creatures are different than I thought they'd be. They stand tall on two legs, fingers drawn out into long black claws and chests that seem to be part man and part beast. But their features, those are all monster. Sharp teeth and snapping jaws meant for howling, meant for maiming, meant for... killing. Their feral eyes glow yellow like moonlight.

A security guard rushes over with a thick club that emanates an ephemeral light that shoots out and stuns the wolves into immobility.

"Confinement, the both of you," the guard snarls. When his hands clamp over their arms, the three disappear into wisps of lingering white smoke.

Charming.

"Give me your schedule." Saint doesn't wait for permission before he's pulling the slip of paper from my blazer pocket with a familiarity that speaks of a friendship that isn't there. I study him and every peeking line of ink that shows just above the collar of his shirt. He looks it over seriously and nods, shoving it into my hands. "Classroom 33. I'm going there, too."

Great. So I'll have to deal with him in class as well.

The day just keeps getting better. Next he'll tell me we get to share a bathroom stall as well as a shower.

The memory of his arching cock flits through my

mind... the shower part probably wouldn't be too bad really if he had a better personality to match his body.

"They probably just threw all of us late admissions together," he explains.

For once in my life, my tardiness has real consequences. Like this vampire who's a little too okay with throwing his dick around.

Literally.

I try to contain my nerves by pressing my hands into the pockets of my blazer and tightening them into fists so they don't shake. It's easy to pretend. I'm good at it.

All around me, bodies jostle my own. They're pushy, the females with the strange, ethereal features of pointed ears and eyes that are too bright to be anything other than mystical. Some of the others, the more unique ones, slip by less aggressively. The ones with webbed hands connected to strangely pointed joints, forked tongues against bulbous chins, red eyes gleaming with the crimson promise of violence, wings and claws, those stand out.

Beings both heavenly and demonic prowl the halls.

I try to appear confident with every step I take. I act like I belong here, like they do. Like my world hasn't been upended, like I have a fucking clue what's going on right now.

The truth is, I know very little about these people. I wasn't raised like them. I was raised to avoid supernaturals. Yes, we all know they exist, but the man who took care of me, he hates them.

And part of me does too.

We stop before a wooden and glass door with the emboldened number 33 stamped on the fogged glass. Saint reaches for the knob and pushes it open.

"Ladies first." He gestures with all the flourish of an eighteen hundreds gentleman. He might as well lift his top hat to me and twirl his fucking cane.

He's so bizarre.

My eyes roll to the back of my head and catch a vivid glimpse of my petty thoughts of the overly attractive vampire. The pettiness doesn't lurk in the back of my mind behind happy thoughts. It sits in the center, in front of the TV and flips back and forth between entertained by the amazing Bob Ross and the asshole standing before me.

The first thing I notice is the smell, it reeks of mildew. It's like the carpeted floors are seeped with mold. Something I feel once my white shoes squish into the material. I sweep my gaze around. Half of the carpet is torn out in strips, as if it had been abandoned in the middle of a renovation. The room overall looks like disastrous shit that doesn't want to be here any more than I do.

Really, the only thing in the room that looks new is the whiteboard, sprawled with large bold lettering that glitters and waves like a magical banner.

INTRODUCTION TO PRODIGUMS 101

. . .

The funding of this place is completely bizarre. My outfit looks like it stole the budget and I'm not even sure why it matters what I'm wearing. Will my monster GPA just completely crumble if I walk in wearing a Jonas Brothers reunion shirt and ripped jeans?

The desks seem sturdy enough, the chairs less so. People are seated two to a table, and it reminds me of human high school biology when I had lab partners. Most every place is occupied by people whose expressions range from solemn, to pissed off, to on the verge of committing mass murder.

Well, at least I know I'm in the right place, I guess.

"You're late!" a stout man accuses. His stiff brown tweed suit reminds me of a children's story book character but I can't place him. His balding head glows under the harsh fluorescent light of the bulbs. He has a smattering of hair behind his ears and on the back of his head. You'd think he'd find a spell to make himself look less like an amphibian. Unless he shape shifts into a frog or something. Seems a little odd, but who the hell knows with this place.

Saint shrugs too casually, almost mockingly. "It seems I am."

Wow. Suddenly he's a bit more attractive than his literal cocky dick lead me to believe.

The teacher goes red in the face. "Tardiness will not be tolerated."

"Oh, don't take everything so seriously. I was showing the newbie around."

My face flames at being referred to as the newbie. He's as new as I am, fucking vampire.

"There are rules to uphold, and we punish tardiness with confinement." The teacher speaks directly at me.

As if it's my fucking fault our juvie dorm is miles away from this building. As if it's my fault Saint said he had to stick to the shadowed parts of the buildings or else he'd burn to a crisp and explode like crackling Rice Krispies—which I later found out he fucking lied to me about. The moment we arrived and sunlight washed over his porcelain fucking skin and there was no combustion. Unfortunately. As if it's my fault no one bothered to explain the rules of this shithole to me.

"Won't happen again," I answer with forced obedience as I make my way to a table at the very back of the room.

"You'll find notebooks and supplies in the closet at the back of the room." Mr. Toad sniffs haughtily as he gestures with a fat, triple-jointed finger.

There seem to be a lot of prestigious students at the academy, a lot of poor ones as well. The school is obviously funding the supplies, and I can clearly see they took the cheapest route. Thin binders sit in stacked rows in the small closet. Plastic things with the stamped insignia of the academy on the cover as if we might be confused about who really owns these. Each one is filled with roughly ten slips of paper. I know because I flick through it the moment I pick one up.

Cheapskates.

I take a pen in a cup and avoid Saint's gaze as he does the same, his wrist bumping mine just lightly. When I take a seat, he slips in right beside me. Like fucking glue I can't get rid of. Like that one smear of paint on a shirt that, no matter how many times you wash it, it just won't come out.

Like shit that just won't rub off the bottom of your shoe.

The teacher, *Mr. Toad* in my mind, clears his throat. "As I was saying, there are three types of creatures in this world: Humans—or fecks as we may call them— are beings with no special significance whatsoever..."

My lip curls at the description. A feck... is that like fuck or frack? Just a week ago, I was basically a fucking human frack, and so far every word spewing out of his mouth is infuriatingly racist.

"... Supernaturals: beings with powerful monsters—or *Prodigiums*—living inside them, contained and living safely among everyone else." He gives a pause as his gaze sweeps around the full classroom, stopping with particular attention on Saint. "And then there's you: the bottom feeder supernaturals who don't even know how to *be* a supernatural."

The pause he lets linger is short lived before he carries on.

"In this class, we will cover all Prodigium creatures, from your everyday feline shifters, to your banshees and burlhorns..."

His tone drones on and on and I'm not sure if I

should waste my ten precious sheets of paper on this or just stare dumbfounded.

I choose the second.

And so my first day at the Academy of Six begins.

I spend the next hour listening to Mr. Toad go on and on about the different types of Prods. Everyone looks bored. Finally, I jot down the different types as he explains them, staring at the words on the pricey little lined page. Perhaps, if I look at one term long enough, then I'll feel a jolt. I'll feel something to indicate, to give me some type of clue as to what lies dormant inside of me. What killed my ex boyfriend?

The thing is, I don't *remember* that day. There's nothing but a shadow of darkness where memories should be, something essential missing in my mind that landed me in this joke of a place. To be honest, I'm not sure I even want to remember. The Prods that arrested me that day showed me pictures of the carnage afterwards. There was nothing left of him but an assortment of limbs, blood and guts. Do I really want to remember that loss of control? Do I really want to know what vicious beast lies inside of me that is capable of completely ripping apart a grown man?

Adam was more of a man baby, really.

The point is, I don't have a fucking choice.

I need to find out what's inside me, no matter how painful the truth may be. Even if it wakes me up in the middle of the night heaving and gasping for breath, begging for forgiveness that I don't deserve, I need to *know* and I need to control it.

Because what happened to my ex can never happen to anyone else ever again.

My heartbeat becomes a loud drumming sound in my ears. I try to focus on anything else, my hand drifting with the pen, twirling with inky colors and lines to distract myself from my own worries.

I'm so lost in my thoughts, I don't realize when class ends, and I'm still doodling against the edges of the page absentmindedly. Claws and teeth, wings, and a disfigured body in bloody remains.

Fuck.

"You're a pretty good artist," Saint compliments, tugging the page of my notes towards him.

I pull it back, slip it into the little plastic binder, and gather my things to leave without a word . I can feel Saint prowling behind me. If I didn't know any better, I'd say he's being purposefully creepy just to make me uncomfortable. Either that or he really wants to drink my blood.

"Mr. Von Hunter, a word, please." Mr. Toad's voice cuts through my thoughts with all the subtlety of a croak. My steps falter, and I hear Saint let out a soft curse behind me before his feet are redirected to the teacher's desk.

I pause shy of the door, my hand poised on the knob to turn it and leave. I should leave. But I'm curious as shit and want to know what he's reprimanding Saint for.

Nosey, nosey.

Why do I even care?

Now I'm the one stalking .

"Just because you come from one of the most prestigious families and one of the original six founders of this academy does not mean you are immune to the rules and punishments."

And there it is.

When I was a child, my father had a cat. A demonic little shit with black fur and yellow eyes that hissed, yowled, and scratched like it was possessed by the devil itself. I liked to watch it. I grew curious at its cruelty and lashed out at the thing myself. I remember one particular moment when I yanked at its tail and the heathen bit me, teeth embedding so deeply into my skin that I bled for hours.

"You knew nothing good would come of it, and still you did it anyway," my father chastised as he wiped my tears.

I'm not sure why this reminds me of that moment. Probably because I know I should *not* have listened to this, and yet I did. And there's no going back from that truth.

Saint's family funded and founded this fucking prison.

And they sent their son to rot in here right along with me. What the fuck did the vampire do to get sentenced here? Is he really that out of control that he risked his family's reputation by getting locked away?

Nerves make my hands tremble as I push open the

door. Saint's response is lost among the cacophony of raucous calls and shouts of delinquent Prods.

I'm completely alone now, left to my own devices to roam these halls and find my next class. The sensation is overwhelming, but being alone is better than being in bad company. And everyone here seems like bad company.

I drag my feet to my next class without incident. On and on my day goes. I share most of my classes with my roommates, but we don't approach each other, rather glare from across mildewy, half renovated, shitty class-rooms. The only one who even offers me a small smile of reassurance is Malek in fourth period, but even he turns away from me to mingle with his own group of friends, other wolves it seems.

I can't wait until the day is over. So far, I've learned nothing of importance, been given no clue as to what could be inside me. Just as the academy starts to feel like a huge waste of time, it's lunch hour and my feet eagerly carry me to the cafeteria.

Finally. I have something to look forward to in the form of nourishment in my belly. Of a warm meal and cold milk. I'm one of those people who always liked high school food. I lived for chicken nugget day.

I can almost taste the crisp of fried bread crumbs on my taste buds as I push past the double doors and come to a screeching, surprised halt.

This... this can't be it, can it? No pleasant aromas warm my senses and settle over me like the hug of an enthusiastic grandmother, who all but shoves food down your throat because *'you're too skinny'*.

Instead, the smells that assault my nostrils are bland. The orderous stench of steam and sweat overpower the food and push the cravings straight from my stomach.

Why had I expected anything more? This isn't grandma's house. It's the fucking Academy of Six, where everything looks like a fourth generation hand-me-down. From the curtains, to the chipped trays, to the stale fucking bread the kitchen staff hands out.

I take a tray and utensils, praying to whatever gods exist that they at least fucking sanitize them, and get in line.

The lunchroom windows are stained with mildew and what... may possibly be blood. They let in just enough mood lighting for depression to really feel at home here.

I swipe a preassembled plate of some sort of porridge type meal, with hotdogs diced up into big chunks, and keep moving with the others.

That's been my goal here, just keep moving and try not to gag at this culinary bullshit on my tray.

So far so good.

Until a mammoth of a hand slams into my tray and the hotdog porridge splatters down the front of my skirt and burns down my calves. Pain sears into me, but the lock of my jaw is a harsher feeling while I breathe though the urge to just completely scream about every fucked up part of this *academy*.

My lashes open slowly on my next cautious breath.

Translucent wings catch the light and the halo around a cruel face with even crueler eyes staring down on me

"Watch where you're going, Feck."

The man's wings shutter with an eerie clicking sound before he rams his shoulder into mine and walks right out, the eyes of this school holding up his ego every step he takes.

Fucking moth man. What the fuck is that? He has bug wings, and that makes him better than me? What are the standards here because Saint's a vampire and he still gets shit on? I bet he wouldn't be such hot shit if I pointed a can of Raid at his sorry ass.

My hands hold up at my sides and for a long moment I have no idea how to react. My lunch, which looks more like vomit, is sliding down my thighs and legs and there isn't a napkin in sight. Can't spare us that luxury it seems.

"Here..." Blonde hair slips into my space before the psycho angel from earlier today falls right to his knees, right in front of me. As if he might start a religion of my body and begin worshipping between my thighs at any moment.

A coldness presses at the highest part of the sticky mess, beginning just below my hem line at the inside of my thigh and he drags the white cloth ever so slowly down. I swallow hard and it's impossible for me not to shift beneath his every move.

"There." His warm breath kisses the quiet word

against my skin before Syko stands to his full height, looking down on me with those sinfully dark eyes.

The small girl at his side rolls her big eyes at the man before taking her tray to a table at the back, her long blonde pigtails swinging with every step she takes.

"Thanks," I rasp out on the weakest sound that pushes from my throat.

"You're *very* welcome." That smile of his shows every one of his perfect white teeth.

He nods to me and I trail after him to where the girl is sitting by the blood stained window.

"Don't fall for it." The girl shovels a spoon of muck into her mouth and I can't help but wait to see if she gags it back up.

She swallows without change in facial expression.

Well. That solves it. This little girl is a demon for sure. Only someone straight from hell could have eaten hotdog porridge and not exorcist vomit right on the spot.

"Don't fall for what?" I ask, pulling out my chair and taking the spot directly across from her. I don't scoot in though. I don't have food and after that warm welcome, I don't think I'll be staying.

The flat out way the girl seems to not give the tiniest hint of a fuck and the annoyance in her gaze when she looks at Syko makes me like her immediately.

Common interests and such.

"Don't fall for that obnoxious flirtation my brother likes to shove down women's throats. Don't fall for it, you're too good." Her round face holds the soft curve of adolescence but it seems something in her has aged her outlook on life.

"No, she's not. She's not too good for it," Syko whispers, his hip leaning right next to me, his palm splaying wide enough to nearly slip his fingers right between mine.

... shit maybe I'm not.

"She is." The girl passes her cold glare back to her brother, and he arches a nearly white brow at her.

"Want to know the secrets to keeping the big bad monsters off your back?" His voice is pure, low drawn out seduction.

And I hate that I truly do want to know the advice he's about to tell me.

I nod hesitantly.

He takes a single step closer, his boot settling with a quiet tap along the dirty tile floor just between my thighs. He interrupts my space just like that, but the closeness is something that draws me in like an unseen power luring me to him. His head dips and I follow the move with watchful attention.

"The secret is," one hand settles on the back of my chair and before I know it, my chin is tipped up to him, breathing in his close spoken words and the gleaming glint in those dangerous dark eyes, "the secret, Innocent Izzy, is to find bigger, badder monsters." A tearing sound tips through the room just as enormous, battered white wings jut out from his broad shoulders. Warmth slips down my cheek and when I look up, each one of those perfect feathers are coated in blood.

His blood.

My breath catches but I force myself to find a steadiness inside me before replying. "And you think you're the bigger, badder monster?"

The way his lips carve up in a sneering smile should be answer enough, but he leans in ever so slightly, his warm promising lips grazing mine as he speaks once more just to me.

"I know I am."

And that is how I became best fucking friends with an angel living a life in hell...

Wait. Stop. Time out. I'm getting too distracted by the one pretty thing in this entire doomsday of an academy.

"What are you?"

The mysterious shine in his eyes brightens and his arms flex from holding himself rigidly above me.

"What do you think I am?" His weight shifts and now he's so close to me his hips are held firmly between my thighs, not touching but blazing up my skin with how much his pants tease my center with his closeness.

"You're an angel." I don't blink, I refuse to show any uncertainty from here on out with these people.

He shakes his head but doesn't answer.

"We're nephilim. My brother and I are children of fallen angels." The girl cuts in like she's absolutely sick of watching the two of us.

"You're one of the founding Prods," I say slowly, trying to remember the notes I took.

Syko straightens slowly, pulling back from me fully as he shrugs and pushes his white hair out of his big black eyes. "It's not really a prestigious thing to be a race of the founding six prods who created this shithole." The venom in his words linger in his cutting features. "The angel, the vampire, the faerie, the shifter, the warlock, and the nephilim had good intentions. They prevented reckless supernaturals from destroying the world. But this place is not what they had in mind. I refuse to believe a daughter of a fucking angel took one look at this prison and said 'sign me up'. It was a great idea with a shitty execution." He slinks down into the chair next to mine and I note how discreetly he slides his arm along the back of my seat.

"What's your name?" The small girl asks.

"Izzy. What's yours?"

Her dark eyes study me for a moment as if she might not tell me at all.

"Kayos." When that strange name slips from her tongue, her pretty blue eyes flicker from bright to black before she blinks it away and focuses on her lumpy lunch.

Nerves crawl through me, the hair along my arm standing abruptly on end as I watch the sinister little girl with the big beautiful eyes.

Syko nudges my leg with his, drawing my attention back to him as he shakes his head just minimally.

"I forgot ketchup," she mumbles on a faraway voice and my confusion only grows when she wanders off to... god knows where because I guarantee condiments cost extra in this joint.

"Kayos is a nephilim startle Prod." Syko's voice is quiet, timid sounding. It's the first time I've ever heard him be so serious about anything since the moment I met him.

"A startle Prod, what's that? And how old is she? She has to be the youngest person I've seen here. Is it even legal for a little girl to be thrown in this prison palace?"

A sad sort of smile pulls at his lips and I have to admit he's handsome in that tragic way.

"She's fourteen. The President of Prodigiums doesn't give a fuck what our age is. Kayos is dangerous. That's why she's here. If she doesn't get her creature under control, they'll control it for her. And startle Prods, they don't stand a fucking chance. Any sudden sound, any threatening setting, any... *any little thing* will set her off. And the people in her path, they're as good as dead."

The way the muscles in his arms bulge when he folds them across his chest and plasters a picture perfect smile on his face tells me she's back. She slides into her chair, ripping open little packets of sugar and shaking them out onto her food without thought of what the fuck that sugary hot dog concoction must taste like.

But I can't seem to even glance down at her tray though. All I can think about is how the supernatural government sent this sweet little girl into the one place that's like a ticking time bomb for her. Syko's right, she doesn't stand a chance.

I can't imagine how it must feel to sit back and watch your own flesh and blood and know that they're going to fail.

A strangling feeling consumes my chest and I just sit there numbly while she eats, her gaze flickering from time to time when a fork clatters to the ground or a tray rattles the metal tables.

With each sudden sound, I can't help but wonder if this is the last thing I'll hear sitting across from the innocent little girl.

But nothing ever happens. Syko does an endless job of making sure she's distracted, focused on his charming words and larger-than-life laughter.

He's... *sweet.*

I think.

Chairs knock to the ground, several of them banging into each other just before an entire table flips and a man with burning palms collides his blazing fist into another demon's face. The two plummet to the ground, knocking more chairs, trays and people to the floor in their tumbling violence.

"Let's go, Kayos." Syko's spine is stiff, shoulders broad and ready. He's a living, breathing defense mechanism in this moment.

Kayos's lips tremble, her teeth sinking in hard to stop the quivering of her jaw, but even as blood trickles from her mouth, she still shakes uncontrollably.

"Now, Kayos," Syko grabs her hand and without another word, his wings splay wide and in the next instant he's soaring her over the deadly crowd at a controlled, casual pace.

The door bangs open in his wake and the sunlight casts across his bloody wings like an angel set out for vengeance.

And I know, that's exactly what he'll be if anything ever happens to that little girl.

SIX

Izara

The afternoon classes fly by and I stumble along with it with so much dread in my stomach I think I might be sick.

Because the last thing on my fabulous agenda is the one thing adults shouldn't have to put up with.

I just shouldn't. I did my time. I ran my miles.

I should not. Have to do. Fucking Gym.

The sunlight prickles my eyes as I glare up at the nicest building this whole damn campus has to offer. Figures they'd throw the budget on something as torturous as this.

Academy of Six Prodigium Gymnasium

The big white letters read.

My lungs premeditatively burn just reading it.

I still have the disgusted look curling my lips when footsteps and hushed whispers crawl up the winding sidewalk to where I stand.

All that hatred flashes away in the next instant.

Pain rivets up my spine when I feel the blow from behind. I have no time to react other than to take in quick, agonizing gasps. My feet almost give out under me, but I'm hauled up by the back of my blazer, whirled, and slammed face first into a wall.

Tears burn behind my eyelids and I force them away with rapid blinks. A meaty hand grips my long hair, pressing my cheek tightly against the rough brick. I can feel the stone abrading my skin but the pain is nothing compared to the rage rising inside.

It rises all at once, uncontrollable, a *familiar* rage that startles me at first.

A body presses against my back and rancid breath burns the hair on my eyebrows as that disgusting mouth gets closer to me, his lips brushing my skin.

"Looks like the academy let in another feck," the deep voice murmurs, causing shivers of unease to race over my arms.

"Get your filthy paws off me, asshole!"

My words might as well have bounced off stone, for all the attention he pays them.

But the way energy is ripping through my chest tells me something bad is coming.

Something from inside me.

Fingers dig into the roots of my hair as he tips my neck unnaturally back. I feel the pain down to my scalp, to my skull. The tears come then from the pain, the rage, a mixture of too many uncontrollable emotions.

"Why do they let scum like you in?" the voice at my ear demands. I can hear the snickers and lewd sneers from whatever companions are at his sides. I can't see them but I know automatically that if my Prod wasn't so deeply buried inside me, I'd slaughter them all.

And the headmaster thought I had no control over the lurking beast.

He's wrong.

I refuse to be responsible for another massacre like Adam's.

With a slow breath, I calm the shaking, deadly sensation within and it quiets in an instant like a soft purring cat nuzzling before falling to sleep.

Good. That's good.

Another hand wraps slowly around the skin of my neck, nails cutting into my throat. The touch isn't lewd, but it holds the promise of violence and death. I feel the first scrape of claws against my flesh and then fingers are wrapping around me, choking me.

I struggle, but he's too strong. A feeling of reckless, helplessness churns within me against this onslaught. My vision blurs black and white. I frantically buck against my assailant, searching deep inside myself for the power of my Prod that I shrugged off too soon.

It's empty, I'm empty.

And I am going to die here.

I can feel myself falling into unconsciousness. I start

to lose myself to the darkness inside. It's all consuming, rising in a powerful threat that wants nothing more than to explode, wreak havoc. I feel it balancing on the delicate edge of my mind, my soul—

And then the feeling is ripped from me as that lashing hand slips away from me and I'm left gasping for breath. Burning heaps of air hit my lungs all at once. My body slumps into the wall and the weakness in my knees has me sliding painfully to the ground.

My attackers, big surprise, are werewolves.

These beasts seem more on edge than the others. Maybe it's a shifter thing. Maybe it's because part of them isn't theirs at all but a monster waiting its turn.

Or maybe, maybe they're just total assholes.

Their claws extend in vicious curves. *Fucker, ever heard of clippers?* Weak hysterical laughter wants to bubble out of my throat as the thought flicks unbidden through my mind.

My fingers tremble at my sides and no matter how hard I try, I can't push the unshed tears from my blurry vision.

But I see it clearly when Wolfie goes down on a thudding slam at my side. Big fists strike, lashing into his cruel face without hesitation. Blood splatters across my cheek and lip and when a boot slams into the wolf's side with a strike of finality, I look up to that blinding white sunlight once more.

To find a soulless demon as my savior.

Nubbie.

Oh, I should not call him that.

Maybe later.

But not now.

His palm wipes over his khakis and a deep crimson color stains the material there. He looks annoyed at the whole ordeal. Usually men enjoy playing the hero. He just looks like he'd rather be elsewhere.

His booted foot slams down onto the wolf's throat, causing him to gurgle, to struggle. His feeble attempts are so pathetic, I feel the need to *laugh into his cruel face.*

But then my savior bends low, so he's crouching over my attacker's body. It happens for a split second, a terrifying moment when those bright green eyes of his go dark, the color swallowed by the black of his pupils. The veins around his eyes swell and darken, as if the blood in his body rushes as black as the pits of hell. His face is spider-webbed in slashing lines that make him look all the more dangerous, deadly.

"I'm an incubus," he mutters with an emotionless voice. "And even I wouldn't put my cock in you." His heel digs into the man's throat. "Though I do have friends in hell who would revel in taking turns to make the werewolf bleed."

The wolf makes a pathetic whimpering noise.

"Consider this your warning to fuck off." He removes his heel and straightens, fully composed once again.

Beautiful, frightening emerald eyes flicker from the wolf at his feet to myself also lying in a mess of a pile near his shoes.

"I'm fine," I croak out in an unintelligible sound of words.

I have the urge to stand.

But I can't move.

"*Christ*," he sighs, shaking his head with annoyance before slipping his hands beneath me. His chest is rigid when my head falls against it. Strong arms and impossible strength surrounds me, warmth and the smell of smoke wraps all around my tired limbs like a protective blanket and I won't lie.

I don't completely hate it.

Until he speaks.

"Listen, Feck, if you're going to be letting these fuckers beat the shit out of you day in and day out, don't do it at the gym. I like the gym. Try to keep it clean there."

Oh, my god he's obnoxious.

Rude.

Condescending.

And completely serious.

"I didn't let anyone do anything to me. I'm fine."

He starts walking in steady strides as if I weigh nothing at all. "Yeah, I could see that." He takes the front steps of our dorm two at a time, jostling me so much I grip his neck harder just to stay safely in his arms.

Smooth muscle tone flexes beneath my fingertips and my fluttering heart notices immediately while my mind pretends she's not impressed.

She's not.

It takes more than an incredibly perfect body to distract me.

Shit, what was he saying?

"Just try to avoid confrontation and you'll make it out just fine."

"This entire place *is* confrontation." My head bangs into his thick neck as he dodges and weaves around two girls ripping each other's hair out in the middle of the dark hall.

Case and point.

Exhibit A.

I rest my case.

Meeting adjourned.

And so on.

"Then I don't know. Find someone to intimidate your intimidators. Otherwise you're as good as gone."

"Like you?" I fire the question back with a glare and pursed lips but then it suddenly sounds like the best idea, really.

Nubbie is massive. Probably because of that gym obsession he has but I'm not really complaining now.

Good for him for bulking up to an impossible size to be my intimidator.

"Yeah, no, not me." His deep mossy eyes pass a disgusted look over me like he couldn't care less what happens to this little feck. And yet, he pulls me closer as he steps carefully over a sleeping black panther curled up just outside our room.

Shifters—shifters everywhere in this place.

I can break him. I can hire him as my intimidator.

I just need a bit more time, here in his arms, where he has to look at my pathetic fucking face and somehow keep saying no.

I will break him.

"Wait." My palm settles on his chest and every part of his body tenses from the way my fingertips arch there over his soundless heart.

He really is attractive in a captivating way. All of these people have this alluring ability to make me want to dive right into the violence they're hiding just beneath the surface.

This guy is no different. He's just more blunt about what lurks on the inside. His jagged exterior and tattered interior all match.

And yet, I'm still stroking my hand down his chiseled chest. His body is sculpted to the point of distraction.

The low state of his brows shadow his wide eyes when he looks to me with, dare I say, some concern there in the depths of his gaze.

"How bad does my neck look? My dad—*my adoptive dad* is supposed to come see me as soon as they allow visitors." My chin tips up and I angle my neck closer to him.

Warm breath trails a heated path along my skin while he hesitantly looks from my eyes to my neck and then back again as if he senses a trap.

He's smart.

Finally, a low rasp comes out from his throat in such a sensual sound that my thighs shift in his arms, his fingers tightening over the bare underside of my legs. "It's pretty sliced up," he whispers. He swallows slowly, attention lingering there on my wounds. "You're weak, Feck. He could have really hurt you." I hear the word feck but it's drowned out by the way his tone is filled with thick concern.

"Then help me," I say on the softest voice I'm capable of. "*Please.*"

"How?" Annoyance stings through him and we're right back to square one again.

Footsteps sound at our side and Saint pushes the door open, appearing as if from nowhere. "Easy, pretend to be her boyfriend." *Had he been listening at the door?* The fuck... "She'll be safe even when you're not around. Safe by association. No one's gonna mess with something that's yours."

Something that's yours.

... I belong to this asshole now? That was not the plan.

"Yeah, she doesn't even know my name so I doubt this lovely couple plan will really work. She hates me." He tells his friend as if I'm not even in the room with them.

"And yet you're holding her the way a groom would his bride." The vampire cocks a dark brow.

Nubbie's arms give out so fast I nearly drop right to the ground. My nails dig into the back of his neck for support and the groan that shakes through his chest is a sound that wakes up my sex drive so fast I have to beat it back down with a broom before I can focus on a single thing either of them are still saying.

"Just date her," Saint says carelessly with a shrug, pushing the subject so hard it feels suspicious.

"I'm not dating her," Nubbie growls with so much disgust I have to remind myself I'm still clinging to him like old toilet paper stuck to his boot.

My hands unlock and I shove off of him with a bit too much force. No one even looks my way when I nearly plant my face onto the floor.

"Then pretend date her," Saint presses.

"No."

"Yes." The vampire's amusement grows with every push and pull of their argument.

"Fuck you."

"Fuck you harder." Saint's smile shines in his bright blue eyes even as his friend is giving him a death glare that his kind must practice religiously with the devil before coming to earth. "You won't date her because you don't know how to do anything with a woman that doesn't involve your cock."

For several seconds the demon just clenches his jaw, aggression rolling off of him in slashing energy that I can physically feel pulsing through the room.

"Fine," he snaps out on a cold, cutting tone. Glaring green eyes span to me and it takes me a second to realize he just agreed.

"Oh, I'm sorry, were you asking me out just then? I'll have to check my calendar, August is kind of a busy month for me." I nod to him and every little shake of my head seems to piss him off even more. "What's your name, Nubbie?" My lips quirk, but I force them not to lift into the taunting smile that's demanding to be let out.

A spasm shakes through his jawline, his head tilting back with a tired look while he glares down on me.

"Phoenix."

Phoenix. That's prettier than I would have expected from a Prod who apparently has no soul.

My hand lifts and he glares down at that little offer held between us. Calloused fingers slide against mine, his big palm settling there for a lingering moment while I shake his hand slowly.

"Nice to meet you, boyfriend."

He blinks an annoyed look of anger at me.

His warmth slips away from me and he stalks out of the room without another word, the door banging shut behind him. I stand there for a moment longer and consider the deal I just made.

I'm dating the campus asshole and he's repulsed by every little thing I do. I can calm him. I know I can. This set up could be good for us both.

If we don't kill each other first.

This boyfriend/girlfriend thing isn't as great as everyone makes it out to be.

SEVEN

Malek

"What do you mean you're dating her?"

It's rare a smirk that tilts the nasty demon's lips.

"I mean she asked, and I said yes," he replies carelessly, pulling himself up to the bar, his massive body flexing with the pull of his muscles as he lowers himself slowly before bringing his chin right back up above the metal bar.

"You're only speaking to me right now to piss me off. And I don't believe you for a second."

"Why? Did you think you'd fuck the pretty feck first?"

Feck. I hate his kind and the way they use that offensive term. He thinks he's so much more powerful, more worthy because he's hellbred.

He's an abomination. Nothing special in a place like this.

"She's not a feck. Don't call her that."

"She's shown zero powers. *She's a feck.* Until proven otherwise." He drops, his shoes hitting the soft mat before a pile of brick and fire land at his feet. He doesn't look up at the damage the man at his side is doing.

It's chaos in this place. It's good she didn't come today. She's not ready. I want to ease her into it. I showed up early to do just that.

And yet, Phoenix was faster.

I should go talk to her. Find out what the hell Phoenix is talking about.

Dating her.

"You're not dating her," I call back over my shoulder as I walk away, not even looking at him as I shove open the metal doors, but I can sense him following behind me at a leisurely pace.

"Maybe. You'll find out when we wake you up to the sound of her fucking orgasms milking my cock tonight."

My fists clench so hard my nails dig into my skin.

Fucking soulless.

It takes everything in me to keep walking, my shoes pounding the pavement as I practically run to Dormitory J.

Why would he say that shit?

He's lying.

She's too smart to be associating with demons. Especially a soulless demon.

The continuous mantra of reassurance circles my

mind as I stride down the hall and fling open our door in a matter of seconds.

She lies quietly on the bottom bunk below Saint, who apparently skipped gym as well. She's curled up on her side beneath a thin white sheet, sweat making her long hair stick to her face as she breathes quiet sounds in her sleep.

"What are you jogging in here like a mutt in heat for?" Saint's taunting words remind me just how good of friends him and the fucking soulless incubus are.

They're both assholes.

"What's with her and Phoenix?" I jut my chin at him and close the door quietly behind me.

"What do you mean?" The vampire's eyes shine with cruel amusement as he watches me and I know he knows exactly what I mean.

Fucking prick.

"Why's he think they're dating?" I don't play around, I'm not into his games. I just want to know what they're doing with her.

Right now.

"I don't think he thinks anything." At the sound of his twisting words I nearly bark at him with the growl crawling up my throat, but he cuts me off. "He's dating her, Malek. Why? Is that—is that an issue for you?"

"He's not fucking dating her. Stop. Stop with the eerie games. Tell me what you two fucks are doing."

Saint leans up on one casual elbow to really speak with me, like we're having the most normal conversation in the world instead of waiting for me to rip into him the moment he tells me whatever cruel plan they're using her for.

"Dogs are so predatory. They piss all over everything in an attempt to claim the whole damn world. You just met her. You didn't have time to hike your leg, little pup." The way that bastard shrugs his shoulders at me has me striding to him so fast, I don't even realize it when I grip his collar and bring his face down to mine, making him teeter on the edge of his bed.

And that demented smile never falters.

His gaze drops and an uneasy feeling churns through me when he glances down at my curled lips.

"Has anyone ever told you," he tilts his head, drawing out his words slowly, "Has anyone ever told you you have a nice mouth, Malek?"

I shove him away hard enough that his back cracks the brick wall.

His smile slices deeper into his amused features as humming laughter shakes through him.

The door swings open casually and the soulless fuck who started all of this glances from Saint to me with a slow shift of his gaze.

"Problem?" He arches his fiery brow at me and my fingers flex into my palm all over again.

"What the fuck are you doing with her?" I growl out, my voice raising more and more the longer I think about it.

"Nothing." Phoenix shrugs.

"Mmmm imagine what she'll be *doing* with him though," the conniving vampire whispers with a suggestive wag of his dark brows.

And that's what sets me off.

My wolf snarls out in snapping teeth, half warping my body in an image of fur and claws before I can stop it. The way the demon tips his head up, offering his neck like he's daring me, courses rage throughout my body.

And then white feathers flash into the room so fast, I don't even see him until big eyes are looking down on me. The angel man from next door pins me to the floor, his gaze wild while he holds me firmly in place.

"Quiet the fuck down over here," he says calmly, his voice a steady whisper.

My palm collides with his shoulder and before he topples backwards, his big wings flutter and he lands with ease on his feet.

All four of us are this rising energy of aggression and I don't see it settling anytime soon.

Not until one of us is dead.

Then the quiet breath of a sensual moan slips from her lips when she turns in her sleep. The sheet slips away, revealing the thin lace of her panties hugging the perfect curve of her ass and all four of us are staring at her.

Quiet settles in. That's all it takes to shut us all up.

It isn't death that we need, it's the perfect, tempting body of one prodless woman.

The tension in my body shifts just looking at her. A

throat clears from somewhere behind me but for several seconds, no one says a single word.

Her white shirt is being held together at the middle by a single tiny button. The soft curves of the bottom of her breasts peek out beneath the twisted shirt and my lips part just looking at her. So much of her smooth stomach is on display that my fingers twitch at my sides with the thought of running my palms down her body.

Fuck, she's beautiful.

So many thoughts slam through my mind at once. The image of those long legs wrapped around my hips, her body arching against me, her head tipped back with complete pleasure—

"I'm going to need you to stop looking at my girl-friend like that, mutt."

And here we go again.

EIGHT

Izara

I'm jolted awake by the dorm room door banging open and smashing against the wall, my delicious dream with Chayanne fading away. Sometimes I think I force the reoccurring dream with the sexy singer and sometimes I think it's just a gift, a gift that I deserve after a day like yesterday.

Before I'm fully awake, I'm hauled from the bed by rough hands.

The blanket that Saint gave me tangles with my long legs, causing confusion in both my mind and my body that promptly makes me stumble to the ground.

I swear, if someone has come to bully me again, I'll gladly let my Prod tear them to pieces this time. They earned a spot on my imaginary hit list for disrupting my dream alone.

The grogginess clears from my vision and I blink away the last remnants of sleep from my eyes to find a school bodyguard looming over me. The sight of his massive frame and jet black uniform covering him from black reflective helmet to big shining boots is terrifying. His whole stature stands at a threatening angle and in his hand he grips his magical buzzing club.

What the fuck?

"Confinement." The guard's voice is little more than a snarl as he reaches out to me.

I scramble away from his grip, panic drills through my chest. "I didn't do anything!"

The commotion stirs my roommates into wakefulness. Slight growls and curses whisper around the darkness.

Dawn hasn't crept into the sky and the moon still shines down on my kicking attempts to escape.

"Don't fucking touch her." Dark rage is in Phoenix's eyes. Pale light slices over his features, but then the guard blocks him out, lunging for me, hand closing around my ankle in a vice-like grip. The sting of harsh magic accompanies his touch, and it pulls at me, tearing me away the moment his skin meets mine.

Images and sound fall away. There's nothing but white noise and darkness and the feeling of panic pressurizing my chest. I'm falling through a void, unaware of how far I'm going until I reach the drop below.

My ass hits something soft and the wind knocks from my lungs all at once.

I blink and everything becomes visible, tangible, again. It takes a moment for the vertigo to subside. Another moment passes for me to realize I'm in a confined room a few inches wider than the length of my arms spread out on either side. There's a small pallet I'm sitting on that's obviously a bed, a thin crisp sheet and no pillow. There's a tin bowl in the corner that reeks of shit.

I feel a small draft coming from a pipe in one of the four white walls. There's no sign of a door, just a barred window that my head wouldn't even fit through.

And peering in through the bars is Headmaster Willms.

His old face is so wrinkled with disapproval he resembles an old, saggy dog.

The fucker.

"Ah, Miss Castillo," the rumble of my name coming from his mouth is condescending. "I was so hoping it wouldn't come to this. And on your first day. Not the best record to start out with." He adjusts the little frames perched on his nose.

I push myself up to my knees in the cramped cage and wrap my fingers around the cold steel bars.

"I haven't *done* anything. Why am I here?"

Dr. Willms sighs. His thumb and forefinger press at the bridge of his nose, pushing at those pretension glasses all over again. "There are rules, Miss Castillo. Rules that everyone must follow if they want to reform back into society."

I'm *trying*. The words don't exactly come out. Just the feel of them in the back of my throat is vile.

"Did you or did you not skip last period gym class?"

Fuck. Everything is clear now.

Gym. The literal bane of my existence right now.

"That wasn't my fault." I rush to defend myself. My neck arches almost unconsciously so he can see the bruising I know is there around my throat.

I had every intention of going to gym—okay, that's an outright lie, but I made an effort. I was attacked right outside of the building. They can't hold it against me, can they?

Apparently they can.

"Classes are mandatory, Miss Castillo. You are not exempt from them, no matter what extenuating circum-stances you claim happened." His gaze barely strays to my neck. He doesn't even care that the wild pack of mutts in this place tried to kill me.

I'm the one being punished for it.

This whole situation is fucking backwards.

"Twenty-four hour confinement," he decides, his voice the gavel banging down. I deserve a defense, I deserve to *explain*.

That matters little to the headmaster. A moment later, he disappears in a swirling puff of white smoke, and I'm left alone with the echoing thunder of my heartbeat.

There's minimal lighting in this place, coming from somewhere I can't see. *Magic*. That's the most likely case.

I sit on the uncomfortable sheet that somehow seems

to be a cross between paper and thin burlap. They didn't even magic me into a pair of jeans. Right. I don't own a fucking thing except for the panties I slept in, dirty black pants, and a uniform covered in hot dog porridge.

Just when I thought Academy of Six couldn't get any worse, they prove me wrong.

And how very wrong I was.

It quickly becomes clear that a person can go mad here. As the hours tick by and I find no comfortable position for rest, my mind wanders. After so long staring at the blank walls, I start to feel like they're closing in on me. Like I'm suffocating.

I force a shaking breath through my lungs and try to calm myself.

I've never feared small spaces, but this place is meant to torture, meant to drive fear in where none should be. Whether it's by magic or my own overactive imagination, I can feel the madness slip in like wisps of slow curling dangerous smoke. Like shadows reaching for feet in the dead of night. Like soft laughter that slowly builds into a crescendo of hysteria until I'm consumed entirely.

That's what this room does to me. It sucks me in until I fall into the darkness of my own nightmares. Sleep brings no reprieve. Not here. Those sweet dreams I had before don't exist in me at all now.

There are shadows and creatures so terrible, I can hardly stand to look at their faces.

In my sleep I flinch away from things I can feel more

than I can see. I'm aware that it's nothing more than a magical induced nightmare, and yet, I can't escape it.

It's all too much.

The hot tears come after the sobs.

And then it's his voice that slices through it all.

"Don't tell me you're scared of shadow illusions? A little dark magic?"

In the dream, my damp lashes slowly lift and there he is. Emerald eyes that look bored as he dusts away crawling shadows like he would a cobweb from his wide shoulders.

The darkness disperses at his arrival. Like it's terrified of him and his power. Like I should be terrified.

Why is it I only feel relief?

"Phoenix?" His name comes out like the exhale of a shuddering and painful breath.

"Was I wrong to assume you were made of tougher stuff than this?" He gestures at my crumpled form.

I'm crouched on the ground, a vast black emptiness surrounds us, but I feel cool solid ground beneath me.

His words strike embarrassment through me so I kneel on trembling knees.

Even if he's only here to mock me, I'm glad for his presence, glad he chased the monsters away.

"Why are you here?" Relief unfurls inside me when my voice comes out steadily.

His eyes flick over me. In the darkness they seem too bright, almost ethereal like a faerie's, as alluring as they are dangerous.

Something about him in this dream seems different. Like his whole body is transformed. Like he's torn away some type of veil to reveal all of his tempting glory. It's not just his body that exudes the thrilling promise of adventure, but the curl of his mouth entices overwhelming desires.

It all feels too real.

A slow burst of wetness between my thighs betrays everything I've felt for him previously. I want him, and the way his nostrils flare as he takes me in lets me know he *knows*.

He takes a prowling step forward, and though I'm sure ten feet separate us, the one step brings him in front of me.

He's standing tall in what was a tiny cage of a cell. It's like this isn't my dream at all, it's his, and he controls what's real and what's not.

My tongue feels leaden in my throat as I swallow back the jolt that threatens to slice through every nerve ending simply from his closeness. His proximity is dangerous, and I'm an idiot for wanting it. My body is so treacherous, it curls against him the moment he's close.

"Your cries of terror called to me," he whispers darkly.

Fuck me.

Please.

Why do those thoughts flitter through my mind?

Oh yeah, because he's an incubus. What did Mr. Toad said about his kind? They thrive off of sex like demons do off chaos. I want to believe I'm strong enough to resist him, but the air in this dream is heady with desire and I feel gloriously drunk on every inch of it.

His hand skims to my lower back and travels against every strand of my long hair. It's like my hair has nerve endings, because I feel the touch of each strand spiral to my core.

His touch has this magnetic ability to change the way I feel about him. That fiery touch makes me want him on the most primal level.

Slowly, he grips a fistful of hair and wraps it around his hand. Once. Twice. Three times until he's near my scalp and pulling at my head so I tilt up to look into those dark, deadly eyes.

My palms fall flat against his chest. His incredibly *bare* chest.

I still in his arms as I realize how very, very naked he suddenly is.

My dreams don't normally progress this fast, but I'm not complaining either.

My palms are seared with every ridge and perfect contour of muscle as they rub up and down.

"I wanted to chase them away."

What's he talking about? My nightmares, right.

I've lost all ability to think in the haziness of my dream that's becoming clearer and clearer the more he leans into me. He's closer to me, his lips hovering a dangerous whisper away.

All I want him to do is close that space between us.

His tongue darts out, slowly slipping against my bottom lip. The wet warmth of that slight touch shudders through me. It burns away all resolve I might have had.

I don't stop to remember who he is. A criminal. A demon. But so am I. Even worse than a demon, I don't know what the fuck I am.

He makes me forget that. I make myself forget as I press my lips fully to his.

But why would I have doubts?

This is a dream after all. The best dream I've ever had.

And the moment our mouths touch, it's like a barrier between us crumbles. Like dreams cascade into a blurred pool of reality. I *want* this to be real.

Is this real?

He lets out a low growl that vibrates through my chest. We devour each other wholly, completely. Our tongues push back and forth. His mouth pressures my own with punishing force. It's like he wants this as much as I do and he fucking hates me for it.

My nails sink into the hard barrier of his skin, and I feel the slow trickling of blood at my fingertips.

The action sets him into violent motion. He releases my hair and slides his calloused hands down the length of my back until he's cupping my ass. I gasp into him as he lifts me up.

It's almost natural to wrap my legs around his waist, heels digging into his lower back.

He whirls and my back meets hard surface. The friction of me sliding up slick panes, of the warmth of his body pressing me against a cold wall, is fucking pure sensuality.

I grip his shoulders for support as his hips grind into mine. The hard thickness of his dick thrusts against the lace of my panties.

And it's suddenly all I can think about.

I want to take a peek. Seriously, he can't magically show up naked and not expect me to be curious.

I tear away from his mouth to look between us.

Holy.

Mother.

Of.

God.

Dream me is setting the bar incredibly high for reality Phoenix.

Poor bastard is never going to live up to the hype of this fantasy cock.

Beautiful, hushed laughter shakes out of his chest and the perfect rocking of his hips halts. "Did you just take a time out to check out my dick?" Amusement curls his lips in a way that makes his features so much softer than normal.

I've never seen him smile. He's always so brooding, so hateful.

He's beautiful when amusement lights up his emerald eyes.

And when I wake up from this, I'll never see it again.

My brows tense and I shake my head quickly. "No.

No. Carry on with your incubus ways." My head tilts, and he meets me halfway when my lips press to his. That addicting rumbling laughter hums along my mouth even as he deepens the kiss with consuming flicks of his tongue.

I want to get lost in his mouth. I never want him to leave. Not when, in some strange fucked up sort of way, I feel perfectly safe right here in this prison of a punishment. Even if my mind is drunk on what he's doing to me.

His big hands cup my ass like they're meant to fit there, just perfectly. His fingers slip lower along the lacy edge of my panties, grazing at my soft flesh. My hips jerk when a finger slips inside and travels up the wet seam of my folds.

He groans. "You're so fucking wet."

And he's kissing me again, his fingers mimics the thrusting movements of his tongue as he dives in and out of me. I ride his hand, craving more friction, needing something else entirely. He bites my bottom lip, then trails a sinful pathway down my neck.

I don't know how he manages, and I don't care. I'm just thankful for the moment he growls out a curse and impatiently shoves aside the material of my panties as if he can't be bothered to take them all the way off.

Like he's as desperate as I am.

I watch, and maybe it's a strange fascination, but Phoenix's eyes stray between us too. Our foreheads touch, our eyes dilating as we watch him lift me just slightly higher.

His movements are laced with hard violence, but he doesn't hurt me. He's gentle despite how much I can tell he's holding back.

I relish in everything he's offering. I relish in the way he poises at my entrance and slowly, ever so slowly, pulls me down on top of him. He stretches every part of me with every hard inch of him. The feel if it pulls the breath right from my lungs and the sharp gasp that slips from my lips lingers between us like it's something to share. His heated attention flicks over my face the moment I cling hard to his smooth shoulders.

That hooded gaze holds on mine, watching me while he fucks me slowly. In a way, with him watching me intently, everything feels heightened. Every rocking move of his hips grinds firmly against my clit, drawing rasping sounds from my lips and bringing the coiling feeling in my core to unbearable heights.

My hips match his slow, drawn out pace and when I work against him just right, he groans into me. His lips brush delicately over mine. It's all a conflicting feeling as his kiss turns sweet and flicking but his cock slams into me harder, pulling deeper groans of darkness right from his chest and passing that sinful sound right into me.

"*Fuck, Izara.*" It's a worshipping tone that's followed by a slow roll of his tongue, sliding his lustful words along my tongue until I feel them build within my chest.

"What is wrong with me?" he growls in confusion. "You're going to make me come."

I don't understand his confusion but I shake my head

emptily at him, pleading to extend the feeling of his cock sliding torturously along my sex before slamming so hard my head hits the wall.

"Don't worry," he whispers with a twisting smile. "I'm controlled. I can control myself, Izzy. I promise." His words make me shiver from the cruel way he says them, taunting but honest.

One big palm trails down my collarbone and he slides the rough feel of his hand across my nipple, pushing aside the shirt almost completely. Dark eyes hold my gaze with that hellacious look before dipping his head low and taking me in his mouth.

The flat of his tongue circles with flicking quickness before sharp teeth rake over my sensitive flesh so hard that I scream. A growling sound of pleasure hums from his mouth and he does it all over again, his teeth meeting my skin at the same time as his cock grinds hard against the most perfect spot deep inside me.

The soft locks of his hair tangle in my fingers and I hold him to me, my head thrown back while my hips work harder and harder against the head of his cock, the sensation building and building and building within me.

Itt all shatters down the middle and rains painful pleasure through me on pulsing waves that clench around him, even as I continue to ride his cock on uneven thrusts until the feeling drifts into slow washing waves.

A slamming sound hits just near my head and his whole body tenses, holding me to him like he's never going to let me go, even as pieces of the wall crumble down into little chunks of rock on the dark stone floor. He holds himself up with one hand pounded into the wall, while still holding me to him in the most gentle way as his release trembles through every inch of his rigid body.

His dick throbs hard within me, making me shift even more against him, which only makes him groan a torturous, sensual growl.

My fingers slide down the sharp angles of his face while his temple settles firmly against my shoulder, his body a solid mass of locked muscles.

It's the strangest feeling of being completely calm and safe in this soulless demon's arms. The warmth of his breath fans over my damp skin, and he never pulls back from me. He lets me ghost across his perfect skin with the slightest touch of my fingers along his jaw.

"When I met you," his tone crawls over the walls like a dark shadow finding its place, "I never would have pictured us like this, Feck." Warm lips press to the side of my throat in a confusingly affectionate way.

"I hate when you call me that."

His head lifts and he just stares at me for a long, long moment, his irises safely back to that warm pine color again. "Tell me what you really are and I'll stop calling you a feck."

My heart sinks but I can't seem to stop touching him.

Even in my dreams he's an asshole.

"If I knew what I was, I'd tell you," I whisper quietly,

sadness tightening my tone despite how hard I swallow the feeling down.

Pain slips into his gaze for a single second and I can't stop myself from telling him even more.

"If you knew what I'm capable of, you wouldn't be holding me like this, that's for sure." I lean forward just because nothing is real right now and I'll be damned if I'm not going to take advantage of it.

I nip at his lower lip, uncertainty still pulling at his features, but he kisses me back anyway, his palms lowering to fully grip my ass again.

"Why do you say that, Iz? I can't imagine not wanting your sinfully sexy body wrapped around mine for any reason," he rasps, his tongue teasing mine slowly.

His obliviousness hurts my heart.

I press the sweetest kiss to that foul mouth of his. "The last man who fucked me got ripped apart by the monster who lives inside this sinfully sexy body." I pause on that thought and he pulls back from my lips slowly at first, and then fully, sliding me down his hard, naked body until my feet gently touch the ground.

That's a good reaction from dream Phoenix. Smart. He's a smart incubus.

But this is my dream. And I need to get the most of it before I wake up to that gym class reality where my adoring boyfriend hates my guts and my classmates want to kill me simply for existing.

My fingers slide through his fiery hair and I push at the back of his head.

"What the fuck are you doing?" he asks, his eyes big with a bit of worry for the first time since I met the cocky demon.

"No one's ever given me head before. I'm trying to subtly get you to go down on me. Is it working?" I ask with a small smile tilting my lips.

"By shoving my head down to your pussy, no. Your subtly sucks, Feck."

A small smirk pulls at my lips and he really is attractive when his asshole gene doesn't sneak up on you.

"Ask me nicely, and maybe you'll get your way," he whispers across my parted lips, my head tipping up to him even as he keeps space firmly planted between us. Slow, hinting touches skim up and down my sides, his fingers trailing all over my body while he waits for my reply.

He's either a powerful incubus or a total idiot for still touching me after what I told him about my past.

Maybe he's a powerful idiot.

"Please?" I nearly kiss him, but he never lets my lips press to his.

"Please what, baby?"

My insides tangle with a wash of heat and desire.

"Please fuck me with that sinful mouth of yours." I arch up against him and his body never moves an inch closer even as I work my mouth along his, his tongue showing my pussy exactly what it's missing while he kisses me so hard I whimper against his lips.

I trust him for some weird reason.

And he must trust me.

Because his head dips lower and lower and lower.

And this sweet soulless incubus spends the rest of the long, dark night keeping me company in the best way possible.

NINE

Saint

He's... *smiling*. In his sleep.

It's... unsettling.

In the last two decades that I've known Phoenix Rutherford, he's never shown as much emotion as he is right now and I know exactly why.

He's dreaming of her.

Is he with her right now? Is he using his demon magic to slice into the veil of her subconscious?

If he is, he has me to thank for that, fuck you very much. I knew this would happen. I don't know what is living inside Izara Castillo, but I can feel it. The darkness of it, the power, it feels just like Phoenix. I don't think she's a succubus or any other kind of lower demon because something like that isn't as quiet and patient as what she is. But they're similar in some way. Maybe she's a hellion with fire coursing through her veins blessed by the devil himself.

She's not a feck. That's for sure.

No feck could make a soulless like Phoenix feel whatever he's feeling right now. Emotions just aren't in him. There's a void inside this man, and she's somehow torn it away and found some fucking happiness in him.

Or lust. Or both.

The smile on his lips shifts, his fiery brows pulling low, his lips parting with a shaking breath that I can almost feel even from across the room right now.

Shit.

What is that innocent girl making my demon feel right now?

His teeth grind together with the lowest groan rumbling through his chest, his fingers arching into his palms like he's filling his hands with... her ass.

I sit up straighter in my bed, glancing to the wolf sleeping on the top bunk across from me before peering back down at the main show currently holding all of my attention.

My dick hardens almost painfully with the next rasping sound that crawls up his throat. A shift of the curtains wafts when I move so fast a sound never even registers in the silent room. That strong, thick throat of his offers up as his head tips back into his tattered pillow.

And then... the hardness of his cock beneath the sheet pulses as dampness seeps through.

"Holy, fucking feck," I whisper with wide eyes held

on his thickness that's still throbbing while his groan echoes around the room.

I've never in my life seen Phoenix actually feel anything during sex before. And I've fucked him first hand.

Nothing.

It's like the emptiness in his heart is just a deep bottomless hole and no matter how many emotions you try to fill it with, it's never enough for him to truly feel anything but hate.

It's the only thing in the world that makes me believe there's a god like my mother says.

There's all this proof that there is a hell all around me. Demons like Phoenix are a surplus here. *Angels.* I've never met one. They're lie for all I know.

But the curses someone like my best friend here is damned with, it just makes me believe that someone out there thinks he should be punished.

I hate them for that.

I hate them for hurting him.

And there's nothing I can do about it.

Big green eyes open slowly, his bare chest rising and falling in rapid heaps of air.

The tensing of his throat makes me wonder just how dry his mouth is for him to keep swallowing so hard like that. His wild eyes shift to me and my smirking face.

"Is the sweet little prodless a good fuck?"

He pushes up from his mattress so fast, I don't even have time to react, until his lips are against mine, tasting me deeply. I can't keep up. Big hands slide along my back and he pulls me down to him, rolling us until I'm pinned perfectly beneath him. The smooth planes of his chest press into mine, his cock grinding into me relentlessly and I thrust against him with more quiet groans slipping between my lips, his fingers fisting my dark hair hard enough to hurt.

I groan against him, the pain building to a demanding pleasure.

Harder and harder he grinds his dick against mine and harder and harder he kisses me, bruising our lips as he seems to search for something.

And then he pulls back, a frustrated breath pushing from his lips, his teeth grinding with the murderous look in his gaze. His head shakes back and forth with agitation growing in him, his palms pushing through his short red hair with a bit too much force.

"She really fucked with you, huh?" I can't catch my breath, but I can't help the excitement spiraling through me either.

I knew she'd get to him.

"She fucking... she made me come, and I felt... I felt everything," His words shake with so much anger you'd think he wasn't talking about how good the Prodless's pussy felt.

"You felt it? Like really felt it?"

He nods.

My fingers glide down the hard lines of his chest and when my palm slides around his thick shaft, he just stares down blankly. With slow strokes of my wrist, he watches, making me so hard it fucking hurts.

His muscles, his dick, the way he moves, and the natural way he knows how to work his body in the best way with someone else's, it's all sinful sexuality and I can't help but remember how good he feels when we're like this together.

But his features never change.

He's erect and ready. But nothing whatsoever happens. Not for him. Not ever.

Except today.

"It was just a dream," Phoenix whispers on a vacant breath.

My touch slips away and if I had a heartbeat, it would be a sad little pathetic sound right now.

Words that go unsaid cling to the surrounding silence.

It was more than just a dream.

The bed shifts hard beneath his weight and he shoves out of the small space, his perfect ass demanding my attention as he flings the closet door open. Slowly he pulls on a pair of khakis, his gaze lost along the dirty floor and the meddled thoughts I can see shifting across his face. One button after the other, he adjusts his shirt until it's hugging the form of his biceps perfectly. He grabs the red tie from the rack and hangs it carelessly over his broad shoulders.

His empty eyes meet mine, jawline set so hard I think it might crack across his flawless features.

"I have to get to Demonology." He grabs a binder off the small square table near the door and with his cock still straining his pants, he walks out.

My head hits his lumpy pillow, a sigh tumbling from my lips.

I knew the pretty little feck would get to him.

It's only a matter of time now.

My eyes close peacefully.

"Why the hell does it smell like a teenager's dirty beat-off sock in here this morning?" Malek growls from the bunk above me, his heightened senses clearly giving away far too much of what he missed out on.

Mmm, that's just the smell of my success.

TEN

Izara

It happens in what I can only assume is the middle of the night. My endless loneliness finally comes to an end. The breath knocks from my lungs and I land on the thin mattress of my bunk with a gasp tearing from my throat.

Muted moonlight pales the room and the first thing I do is look up at the incubus across from me. The vivid dreams were so real that I can taste his mouth against mine, his dick buried so deep inside me I can still feel him there.

But he's sound asleep now. Not thinking of me at all, I'm sure.

I wonder if he worried about me, thought about me the way I strangely thought so much about him.

It's a stupid thing to consider. He's not my real boyfriend. He'd be a terrible real boyfriend. He's a shitty person in general, so it's only natural to imagine him as a shitty friend, partner... lover.

Then why I am I still thinking about him?

He did something. I don't believe those dreams were just innocent—incredibly dirty—dreams.

Is the incubus really powerful enough to somehow control or manipulate my unconscious mind?

I arch an accusing eyebrow at the peaceful sleeping demon.

I'll have to be careful around him from now on.

Not just when I'm awake, I guess.

Springs groan under shifting weight. Movement shuffles in the darkness and then a lean body covered in swirling black lines slips down from the bunk across from mine. Malek's dark hair and amber eyes look completely black in the shadows of the room. He holds his finger to his lips before bending down to meet me at eye level, his boxers sliding up his strong thighs as he kneels there.

"Scoot over," he whispers, his accent cutting into his deep masculine voice.

The pull of my brows is just the start of my confusion because the moment I shift, a gorgeous, half naked werewolf slides into bed with me.

Wow. These dreams of mine are really getting elaborate.

But I'm not dreaming. I know I'm not because instead of kissing me senseless, he keeps his hands sweetly to himself, his body heat washing over me and surrounding me with that scent of deep pine. He's close, but not touching. Respectfully so.

"What are you doing?" I lie flat on my back, looking up into the shine of those dark whiskey-colored eyes.

"What's the deal with you and Phoenix?" he asks with so much seriousness in his features that it's unsettling.

Instead of searching for a real answer to give him, the memories of my dream flood into me and heat creeps over my cheeks until it's hard to pretend to breathe rationally.

Little clips of air meet my lungs and I try my very best not to sound like an orgasmic, breathless idiot. "What do you mean?"

He shifts at my side and tries again. "He said you were dating. Why would he say that?"

Right. Dating. Kind of.

"Phoenix protected me yesterday. Several people keep telling me I'm weak here. I'm not. I'm not fucking weak. I'm...careful." My head shakes at how off track I'm getting. "I need someone like Phoenix to help me. Not only to protect me from the others but..."

His thick brows lower over his pretty eyes. "But?"

"But to protect them from me," I whisper so quietly the words barely come out.

His fingers lift and just faintly, his fingertips skim along my hip.

"What'd you do to get here, Izzy?" There's so much concern in his rasping whisper, the sound of it making me shiver with the feel of his touch gliding back and forth along my skin just above my underwear.

I've never lain with a man like Malek in my entire life. I lost my virginity to a human last year before I graduated high school.

Adam did not look like Malek one little bit. He was a boy in comparison.

And speaking of Adam.

"I hurt someone. I hurt him bad." A tremble of a different kind consumes me as images of Adam's severed head flicker through my mind.

"Shit." His palm splays wide across my stomach and I force a steady breath through my lungs.

"I don't remember it. I grew up in the human society in the city, and I always knew there was a beast inside of me, but I have no idea what it is." My gaze holds his and he just lets me fall apart in his arms for a little while in the darkness away from everyone else. "That's the worst part. Not knowing. Not knowing if I'll hurt my enemies, or the people who get too close, or even myself. That's why I need Phoenix. I just need him to keep everyone away."

Even you.

Malek's sweet. He's kind and caring. And it's dangerous for me to get too close.

And yet, here I am, snuggled up against his smooth, hard chest and pouring my heart out more and more with each ticking second that slips by.

"I know what you mean." His head settles on my

pillow, his gaze trailing along my features while his big hand sweeps back and forth across my ribs, inching beneath my haphazardly buttoned shirt, but never veering too high. "I don't know what you are, Izzy. It's hard for me to want to help you because I could hurt you too. I don't think you're weak, but I know I'm reckless. The full moon is in five days. Stay far, far away from me then, okay?"

I nod slowly but my gaze catches on the fullness of his lips.

He has nice lips.

"You should get some sleep," he whispers, and the moment his body shifts to leave, my hand settles over his.

"I've slept for twenty-four hours." At the sound of my words, he lingers there in my bed. He hesitates for so long I can't help but wonder what he's thinking.

"Slip your clothes on." His feet never make a sound as he sneaks to our closet and starts tossing a uniform at me. "I want to meet your beast. In a controlled setting."

The small smile on his lips dissolves with my next serious question.

"One where you won't lose your arms, head, or cock?"

His lips part and suddenly, the big bad wolf doesn't seem so sure of himself.

ELEVEN

Malek

The woods surrounding the academy provide enough cover for the two of us. The skeletal black trees press together in maze-like rows here. We're far enough into their density that we can't be seen.

I prowled these woods all night last night, alone with the madness inside. Bringing her here seems intimate in a way I shouldn't even allow. I should stay far away from Izara, but the wolf in me wants to claim her. The primitive beast has no qualms about hurting, claiming. I try not to give into it. I don't want to give into it. My Prod and my mind war against each other and neither come to a fucking solution. So I stay away enough to not harm her. But get close enough to torture myself with my own desires.

Like right now.

Every tree is bare of leaves. Moonlight shines in silver

beams through arms and branches, slicing shadows across her features and sinuous movements.

She's seductive, and she doesn't even know it. Some of her beauty is hidden behind pinched brows like she's always carefully picking apart actions, playing the safe side.

And now I know why.

She looks at me with hope in her dark eyes. It's those hopelessly romantic brown eyes that change depending on the lighting. They could be black or brown or as golden as honey in the sunlight.

Right now, they're as dark as night, and I try not to lose myself in the depths of them. In the depths of her.

I've been controlling the beast inside me for five years, since I turned fifteen. I'm familiar with the force of will it takes to push down rage and violence. But my heart has no fucking idea it shouldn't fall completely.

My heart, it's weak. I grew up in a small pack on the quiet countryside in upper New York and not one girl has ever stolen, owned, or broken my heart.

Which is all more the reason to keep that distance between myself and the reckless girl I'm walking side by side with.

"So now what?" She kicks at a stray rock, her gaze flicking over our surroundings. If she's afraid of the darkness, she doesn't show it, but her lips purse tightly.

My arms cross against the span of my chest, an assertive unconscious gesture of dominance that my brothers always hated. She takes in my stance with dilated pupils, her tongue slashing across her lower lip.

Fuck, that's not the reaction I want. Or is it? Isn't that why I brought her out here in the first place? Because I want her to want me?

Yes. But I also want to be her friend. And she looks like she could use a fucking friend. A girl like her shouldn't have to rely on an asshole incubus to protect her.

"Now we bring out your Prod."

A Prod that could tear my head and my cock off if it appears...

My palm shifts protectively over my dick and then, as an afterthought, I wonder why I'm not more concerned about my skull and brains rather than my manhood.

My priorities might be off just slightly.

Her eyebrows raise and a mocking expression presses her beautiful features. "It's not like I haven't been trying to reach my Prod or anything," she finally says.

I push away the sarcasm as I prowl towards her, my boots stomping into the dead earth until we are face to face.

"Picture it," I demand, pressing a finger to the center of her chest, feeling the sudden frantic beating of her heart between her breasts.

Shit.

Don't think about her nipples. Don't you fucking dare.

Too late.

"Don't think of your Prod as a separate entity inside you. As we all know that's not what a Prod is. Think of it as it should be: the darker part of yourself. Your fears and your desires. Every savage thing you've ever wanted. Embrace that, and you'll feel that part of you come to life."

She licks her lips slowly and the sight of it makes my cock go hard as I picture her mouth around me, sliding up and down...

"Is that how you learned to keep your wolf in line?" Her voice is a raspy, heady sound with—dare I think it? —desire.

I pull my hand away from her and force myself to take a step back. *Distance*, I remind myself. Otherwise it'll get too dangerous for the both of us.

"I'm still learning," I confess. "However shitty this place is, there are *some* teachers willing to help. There's good advice here buried beneath all the bad."

She cocks her head to the side as she contemplates what I've said and then her lip catches between her bottom teeth.

"I—" she breaks off, swallows. "I don't know what my deepest desires are."

More like she doesn't want to admit them to me.

Fine. We all have secrets.

"Close your eyes."

Izzy is too fucking trusting. Her thick, dark lashes flutter closed.

For a second I just stare at her and the delicate curve of her jawline, the slight parting of her full lips.

My throat clears in the silence.

"Think back to the moment your Prod lost control. Who are you with?"

She replies tentatively. "Adam."

Just hearing another man's name on her perfect lips makes that irrational beast inside me want to fucking murder someone. I take a breath to calm the wolf down and remind him we barely know this girl.

Within me he snorts pretentiously in response, like it's my fault two whole days have passed and we're not already trying to have a litter of Prod pups with his mate.

Mate?

I clear my throat once more and try to focus on helping her. "Where are you with Adam?"

"At—at his house…"

"What does the room look like?"

Her breath comes out shakier, but she tries. She struggles to answer this for a moment as her brain tries to remember. "He has a twin bed with Star Wars sheets…"

A soft snort that I can't help, pushes out of me. *Was she dating a man or a boy?*

"There's a picture of us on his dresser, from when we went fishing with his family, and an oil galaxy painting I made him is in a little blue frame on his desk."

"What are the two of you doing?"

"M-making out… Malek, I don't think…"

My voice cuts through her protest. "Is he touching you?"

Fuck. I'm not entirely sure I'm asking for her benefit anymore, rather my own. If she hadn't already killed the bastard, I'd rip him to pieces.

Calm the fire, I remind myself. Control the beast.

I shake my head at the chaos that's spinning around in my body.

"He's grabbing my chest and his hand is in my pants, if you really must know."

"Are you enjoying it?" The words nearly come out a snarl, one I try to bite back only to realize I can't. I'm pissed, and the Prod is taking it as an invitation to rip through me.

This is getting out of hand.

I breathe in, out, willing the lengthening of my claws to turn back to fingernails.

It's not fucking working.

Fuck, this is a bad idea.

I shouldn't have brought Izzy out here.

The woods, the rage, it's all clashing together now to set me into a state of mind that I try so damn hard to contain.

This out-of-control feeling, this is what got me into this academy in the first place.

"Surprisingly, no. I am not enjoying it," she whispers, interrupting my memories and my rising aggression.

This stops me cold. The beast, everything in me pauses at her carefully placed words.

"Why not?"

"I was going to break up with him."

Everything stills and the savage part of me spirals right back into the darkness where it came from.

"Why?"

Izzy shrugs and her eyes slowly open. "Because he was awful in bed. Seriously, I had a better time jerking off than I did with him. Awful in bed, awful in conversation, just... awful."

The breath I am about to inhale catches painfully in my chest. Strangled noises come out of me that aren't words but they're not beast either. It's incoherent, and I'm suddenly imagining Izzy lying in her bed. Izzy naked. Izzy with her fingers sliding down the dip between her thighs to touch herself.

Would she like it slow or fast? Gentle or rough? Did she want to be worshipped? I'd worship her. I'd worship every fucking inch with my tongue and teeth. I'd whisper secrets across her flesh of all the naughty things I want to do to her, like take her from behind.

Maybe I'm more beastly than I want to admit.

Maybe my Prod is on to something and we should claim Izara Castillo right here under the moonlight.

"Are you done with the interrogation on my sex life, *pervertido*?"

Pervert. Great.

At the moment, she's not wrong, and she hasn't even seen the things my beast wants to do to her.

We are getting fucking nowhere and it's all my fault.

"Close your damn eyes." I ask the next question when she does. "Describe what happens next. You can leave out the dirty details."

I just might murder someone if she doesn't.

She sighs and launches into her story. Her voice is full of wariness at first as she picks through bits and pieces, describing what she remembers. She tells me how she wanted to give him one last chance but it didn't feel right. Then the timbre of her tone changes, her voice rises and I smell the fear, the hopelessness before it hits.

"And then—I—I—I don't *know*. There's too much, and I'm suffocating. I can't *breathe*. He's—I'm—" Her eyes shoot open in panic and she whispers one word that sends me hurtling towards her right before she drops to the ground. *"Malek."*

I reach her before she hits the dirt and cradle her body to my chest. Every inch of her is trembling like she's having a fucking seizure. And I'm helpless to stop it.

I push her hair from her face and turn her sideways. *That's what you're supposed to do when someone has a seizure right?* But this isn't normal. None of this is fucking normal.

We're not normal.

"Izzy." I hope my voice doesn't betray the fear burning in my gut. "Izzy wake *up*." She doesn't, and I curse. I try everything. I speak to her softly and because I don't know what else to do, I sing softly to her in Spanish like my mother used to do with me and my brothers.

It's the only thing I can think of.

She's okay. She's fine. She's going to be okay.

Fuck.

After a while, her trembling subsides, and when she slowly opens her eyes, I see they're bloodshot in the darkness. She gifts me a tentative smile that slices through the tangle of dread inside me.

"I love that song," she whispers.

"You scared the shit out of me."

She pushes up in my hold, remaining close so her cheek rests near my shoulder.

I inhale the scent of her, the dark traces of fear that still cling to her like sweat. I want to wash the stench away. I want to pull her close, but the beast in me is already too out of control with how fast my heart's pounding and refusing to come down.

I extricate her from my body slowly and help her stand. When she doesn't sway, I put distance between us. As if those three feet would make me less aware of her presence, of the way she felt in my arms. Like she belonged.

"I don't remember, Malek," she says finally with a little embarrassment. "I'm starting to think I never will."

"I'm sorry." I'm breathless because I want to hold her in my arms and never let her go. Because I want her to feel safe and protected.

But I'm a criminal with an out-of-control Prod. I can't fucking protect her. I can't even help her protect herself. I was a fool for thinking I could try.

"Let's go back." I walk away, leaving her to follow.

I'm aware of her every labored breath, every footstep, and the scent of confusion swirling around her.

This is a mess and now both of us are confused.

At least one good thing came out of tonight.

Either what had happened has left Izara so traumatized that she's forcing away the memories, or her Prod is making her forget.

And I intend to find out which.

TWELVE

Izara

Attempting to lure out whatever beast is inside me last night was a cakewalk compared to the torture this morning. Having to look Phoenix in the eye after having multiple orgasmic wet dreams about him... that's just a new awkwardness that I didn't even know I was capable of.

But he and I both know what he did.

Now lets see if he confesses, grovels, pleads for me to forgive him for crossing a line within my dreams.

Even if I did jump his dream dick the moment he stepped foot over that little line.

"Morning," he says in a clipped, careless tone as his body slips from his bed and he walks over to the closet.

... Doesn't sound very grovel-ish.

I wait, but he doesn't add any crying words onto that single phrase...

His hair is plastered to his head on one side, while the other stands out in all sorts of odd directions. He yawns and stretches with a prowling ferocity that makes his muscles ripple with every sexy move. It isn't fucking fair that he can look as attractive as a Greek sex god this early wearing absolutely nothing at all.

He busies himself by slipping on his tight white shirt, long fingers buttoning it up while never meeting my eyes and thankfully never seeing the deep flush of my cheeks or my glaring eyes.

I just can't help but have so many dirty memories of my dreams flash through my mind when I look at him.

I feel like my body is on fire and my cheeks are the only surviving part of me that's trying to warn everyone of the death by embarrassment that I'm experiencing.

"Mornnnggg," I mumble out a string of syllables that almost sound like a greeting, almost sound like a disease.

That gets his steady attention. He arches an eyebrow at me for less than half a second before going back to getting dressed.

I stand from my bunk and linger at the end of the bed near the closet.

He ignores me mostly, shakes his head and turns for the door.

"Don't forget to walk your girlfriend to class," Saint chirps, lording over all of us from his top bunk and watching the show with big, excited eyes.

His strangeness seems to have intensified since I've been gone.

Malek passes the vampire a glare before continuing to water his herbs on the windowsill, forcefully ignoring us it seems like.

Phoenix's gaze drops to my legs, trails over my underwear, and Malek's shirt. It's soft and smells like him and the dirt we practiced in the night before. I don't have any casual clothes, really. I'm tired of sleeping in button-down shirts. Malek was nice enough to literally give me the shirt off his back and he might be the one person I really trust in this place.

The demon's emerald eyes glint until an inky color swirls there at the sight of the baggy shirt hanging on my body.

He blinks the darkness from his eyes.

"You're not even dressed yet," he growls out, gripping his binder and seeming like he might make a break for the door again at any moment. Then he lifts his hands impatiently. "Take Lassie's fucking shirt off and let's go."

His tone alone causes a stubbornness inside me to rear up and demand that I push him even more.

I face him fully and simply cock my head at him.

Then warm fingers slide over my hips just as a strong body presses to my back. Malek's scent surrounds me, his palms teasing over my ribs as he pushes his shirt along my body, halting just beneath my breasts. His big body turns, shifting me until I'm facing the closet, shielding me from the rest of the room as he pulls the material fully off and lets warm air pebble my nipples.

Or maybe it's just because his body is still pressed in

all the right places against me, his breath kissing my neck as he whispers in my ear.

"I'll leave this on your bed for you," he says, his lips brushing so lightly along my ear that I arch my neck for him.

My fingers tremble as I grab the first small shirt I find and I pull it on without thought, my skirt following. They're clean now, no sign of the culinary disaster or stains in sight.

When I turn with my red tie in hand, Phoenix's rage is still ticking through his jaw.

"I'm ready," I beam with the biggest eat shit smile I can muster.

With jerking motions he grabs my binder and shoves it hard into my chest before swinging open the whining door. "Let's go."

A weird happiness flutters through me.

Maybe it's just a natural hate Phoenix has for Malek. Or maybe, just maybe, he's possessive of me. Jealousy even.

I rush after him down the hall and can't help but push him a little more and a little more until even I know I should shut the fuck up.

"Are you mad, baby?" I purr at his side but it does the opposite because then the sound of his sexy tone from the other night is echoing through my mind.

Please what, baby?

Shivers wreak havoc through my body, his voice haunting my mind as well as my sex drive.

"I'm not mad," he says on a voice that, if I'm not mistaken, sounds incredibly mad. "Just some advice. If you want this shit to be convincing, if you want a fake boyfriend, don't let dirty dogs paw all fucking over you then." We storm outside, him pounding his boots over the pavement and me stomping my little tennis shoes even harder to compete.

"Convincing?" My head rears back rather dramatically but I just don't fucking care. "According to Saint, and I'm starting to agree, you wouldn't know how to be someone's boyfriend if a fucking Rom-com smacked you in your demonic face."

"What the fuck is a Rom-com?" He glares down on me, insulted by my use of genre lingo.

"A romantic comedy. The staple of chick flick love." I arch an impatient eyebrow at him, but he just shakes his pretentious head at me. "The point is, if this fails, it's your fault. You only know how to screw women, you have no idea what it looks like for a guy to actually like a girl."

He drops his black binder to the grass and then his hands push low down my back, pulling me close even as my arms hang rather confused at my sides.

"What are you doing?" Why do I keep asking this over and over again in this weird fucking school?

His head dips low, his lips hovering over mine like his next growling words will suffocate me on contact.

A girl from my Prod Health class passes and smirks knowingly, forcing me to smile the most awkward smile that's ever tensed my lips.

"What the fuck are you doing? People are staring," I tell him on a hushed yell.

Then his lips press to mine. Once. Twice. Three times and my hands instinctively clunch his strong shoulders, digging in until there's no space between his hard body and my mine.

"Just showing them what it looks like when a guy likes a girl," he whispers before sliding his tongue so slowly over mine, I can remember the taste of my orgasm on his lips before he fucked me senseless in my dreams.

Lust and embarrassment slam into me all at once at that thought.

I shove out of his arms.

A safe foot of space separates him from me, and he gazes at me with the cockiest smirk on his perfectly kissable lips. I hate his mouth.

That's not what you said last night.

My consciousness is a cruel bitch.

He shifts his weight slowly, picking up his binder, meeting my attention with the most arrogant look on his face. He's so big that when he takes a step forward, he shadows over me, stealing away the hot morning sunlight.

"Let's go to class, baby." His hand slips slowly into mine and with one small tug, he pulls me away from the watchful eyes of our peers.

"Oh, so I'm *baby* today," I mock, knowing full well I should really, really shut up.

But his tone isn't cold and cruel like it normally is. It's

easy and teasing in a way that I'm not used to. "Just for today, Feck."

My lips quirk at the familiar name. That's better.

Hand in hand, he weaves us effortlessly through the crowd. And the crowd? They part for him like a god walking among mortals.

He really is this powerful Prod whose energy can be felt before it's seen. I'm in awe of him, really. It's sad he doesn't seem to have any kind of happiness, any kind of pleasure in this life.

I can't stand not knowing why.

"Why are you here, Phoenix?"

We pass a couple, a *real* couple, and Phoenix's attention drops down to how the male faerie is carrying his girlfriend's binder, book, and purse even.

A short pause drifts through him before he reaches over me and steals my binder away, carrying it on top of his and continuing to lead me into building A. He doesn't mention the binder situation but I can't help but glance down at them every couple of seconds.

It seems you *can* teach an old demon new tricks.

Demon see, demon do.

Okay. Okay. I'm done.

"Last month, I was brought in for excessive theft."

The word *excessive* seems odd but I ignore it.

We reach the Introduction to Prodigium's classroom and I pause there, my hand left forgotten in his.

"Theft? You were thrown into this Prod prison because of theft?"

He shifts on his boots, a strange smirk tilting his lips. He leans in until hardly any space separates us. "I broke into a Viagra warehouse and consumed a pallet of their merchandise."

I blink at him. The exasperation never fades so I'm left blinking at this beautiful man who just confessed his sins of robbing a warehouse and eating what I can only image to be several thousand tablets of Viagra...

"Did your fucking dick explode?"

Laughter shakes out of him in the quietest sound of amusement. It carries until I too, am smiling up at his strange, beautiful happiness.

He shakes his head slowly.

"No, but when I fucked the guard for twenty-four hours straight, his boss called the police. And unfortunately, supernaturals got involved. Academy of Six got involved. I just—I wanted to fucking feel something. *Anything*. I'm an incubus born without a soul. Two opposing natures in one. I don't think it's something they're going to be able to teach me here. You can't fix something that was born broken." The sadness of his tone steals my breath away and I realize we're still leaning into one another, both of my hands holding his now in the most casual way.

I hate the pools of tragedy that have taken over his deep emerald eyes.

He's right, there's nothing anyone can do about who he is as a person.

But I can try to take his mind off of it.

At least for a minute.

"Can I kiss you like a girl who likes a boy?" My head tilts up higher, my nose skimming along his, waiting for his reply with too much emotion pounding through my heart.

His head barely nods before my lips press to his, his body covering mine in an instant, slamming my back into the concrete wall. The slow way his head tilts, the deepness of his kiss, and the faint hint of a groan that hums from his lips, makes me almost think... he does feel something.

But it's all just hopeful nonsense.

He steps back slowly, breath shaking through his lungs like it never fully hits as he stares at me with wild dark eyes, the hint of the demon who owns him peering out through that sinful gaze.

"I'll meet you at gym class." His fingers stall, intertwined with mine for another few seconds before slipping away. "No one will hurt you, okay?" There's so much concern and kindness in his eyes, I don't even know what to say to him. I nod vacantly.

It's oddly easier for us to talk when we're yelling and fighting.

Maybe it's just easier for me.

Maybe I'm the one who doesn't have a clue how to be someone's girlfriend.

THIRTEEN

Izara

"I told you he's a good boyfriend," Saint sing songs the moment he takes a seat at my side.

"You literally said he only knows how to use his cock when it comes to women." My gaze collides with his amused expression.

"That doesn't sound like something I'd say." His ridiculous smile widens to reveal his sharp teeth and I can't help but roll my eyes at him.

"I thought vampires never forgot." I place my binder on the desk in front of me. I'm not looking forward to the day ahead, not when at the end of it I'll have to suffer through fucking gym, but at least Phoenix's presence will ward off the bullies. A small blessing in this shithole.

"The saying is an *elephant* never forgets... I don't know what offends me more, the fact that you basically called me an animal or that you actually take notes in this fucking class." He looks at my carefully scrawled information on Prods with barely concealed disgust curling his lips.

"Just because you're a slacker doesn't mean I have to be." Seriously, even Phoenix takes notes to class. Saint doesn't have a fucking thing. I wonder if he has a good memory and doesn't need to take notes, or if he's trying to purposefully get kicked out.

This place is terrible, but the alternative isn't any better. What could this man's life have been like before he came here for him to be so callous?

"At least I didn't get caught skipping gym."

Of course he has to remind me of that. Thinking of confinement just reminds me of my sex dream with Phoenix, which just makes me blush and causes heat to pool between my thighs as if he were here. Seriously. I can still feel the lingering of his touch over my every inch, and I can't possibly fathom why I'm craving the real deal. He hates me. I hate him.

Maybe we could hate fuck.

Did I say that out loud?

A beat of terrifying silence slips by without Saint's ridiculous commentary.

No. Good.

"They knew about that kind of fast." My foot shakes beneath the table, bumping into his. "It's this ankle bracelet. I bet it has a magical camera and audio built in."

Saint chuckles and in one quick, languid move, he brings his legs on top of the table in a relaxing pose, one ankle crossed casually over the other. The uniform leg of his pants slides up to reveal a pale ankle, and the glowing electric band wrapped around it.

"Not a built in camera," he supplies. "It's a basic nice 'ol magical GPS." His fingers go to it, and if I expected it to burn him, it doesn't. But as he tugs it, the confines only tighten around his skin until it looks like it'll chop his foot entirely off.

Note to self: do not tamper with the bracelet if you enjoy having two feet...

"Only the teachers can take them off, and since most of them want to see us fail, you won't catch one of them coming to your aid." He drops his feet back to the floor with a loud resonating sound. His elegant features pull into tight mocking displeasure.

"So why would they bother with the academy? The purpose of this place is to make us better Prods, better citizens. Now it's a fucking prison."

Saint shrugs, drumming his fingers along the edge of the table. He has a restless energy inside him that comes out in distracting bursts sometimes. Annoying but charismatic all at the same time.

"Times change." The drumming stops and is replaced with incessant finger tapping. I wonder if he's annoying on purpose or if it all comes easy for him. "Nowadays, they don't want to deal with us anymore. Most dangerous Prods leave here just to cause problems in society all over again. It's easier on both their time and budget to try and break us in the first semester instead of reforming us." He stops and gives me a side-long, conspiratorial look. "You know what happens to those who can't reform, right?"

"They go to the real prison." Which is probably better than this place. At least I'm sure they get edible meals. No hot dog porridge for those lucky Goldie Locks.

Saint scrapes his nails along the surface in front of him. "Something like that. Depends on their resources. Look, I don't wanna scare you, but you need to figure out what your Prod is and fast. When the Prodless can't reform, they give them the death penalty in the end. It's too dangerous to have uncontrollable supernaturals among humans and the others."

Unease ripples through me. Fucking what? No one told me that.

"How do you know?"

"Family connections. Family history too. Von Hunters have a bit of a bloody background if you know what I mean." That charming, deadly smile slashes across his features.

Right. He's a vampire, but he came from the founding fucking fathers of this hellhole.

He's likely safe from death, at any rate. Which explains his carelessness.

I take him in, the long length of his body. He's lithe, but strong. His uniform is askew, like he couldn't be bothered to put himself together for this joke of a school, even if his tie is perfectly knotted. Dark hair presses against his temples, curling at the ends and at the back of his nape.

If I had to draw up the image of a prep school bad boy, Saint would be it. With mischief shining in the blue depths of his eyes, and the slightest hint of tattoos peeking out from his sleeves and neck. I can picture him with a cigarette hanging out the side of his mouth and smoke clouding my better judgment, making me actually *want* a taste of him.

He's rich but in a way that money means nothing to him. Just like this place.

"Why are you even here?" I whisper almost angrily. Seriously. He talks back to almost every teacher and yet no one throws his ass in confinement. He does it for the pure joy of annoying them, pushing them to test how much of his bullshit they'll take before they snap. I have to wonder if he even really belongs here or if he pissed off mommy and daddy and this is just some weird rich boy punishment.

All motion in his body stops. A preternatural stillness sets over him in a way that's so eerie, it settles a prickling sensation across my skin. He's a predator, a vampire, and he looks every inch of it as he slowly turns and smiles at me, revealing the jutting points of his incisors pressing into his bottom lip.

"Why do you think?" His voice drops low, and his body suddenly angles closer to mine. I tense, and all I can stare at are those two pointy teeth piercing his lip, drawing a thin line of blood down his chin.

"I don't know." My voice is calm even if I'm all too

aware of the pounding of my heart and the rushing of my blood. "That's why I fucking asked you."

He blinks and throws his head back as he barks out his laughter. When he looks at me again, his teeth have slid back up to their normal size. Really, I'm curious about them. Do they suck blood up like a straw or does he have to taste it? Do the teeth go up into his gums or do they grow like claws on a werewolf? What's the average fang size for vampires? Do male vampires lie about their length or is it not as idolized as other body parts?

The questions are endless but I refrain from spewing my endless curiosity for now.

"No need to worry, I didn't suck the blood out of innocent virgins, if that's what you're thinking."

"Then what did you do?"

"Hmmm didn't contradict my virgin comment. Interesting."

"It's not interesting because I'm not a virgin," I fire back at him and the intrigue in his eyes almost matches mine. But I keep pushing him, "What'd you do?"

"Failed my family," he says quietly.

There is such sadness laced in his simple words, I'm taken aback. It's so raw, so broken, I have this maddening urge to take his hand in mine and offer him some sort of comfort.

"How?" The word is a weak whisper that leaves my lips. All the playfulness in our banter drains away with each ticking second.

I almost think he won't answer me. Maybe I hope he

doesn't. *Think of the devil cat and consequences of actions.* Do I really want to know this truth? It could be harder than I can probably bear.

Eventually he answers me. And it's not in the way I expect at all.

"I failed them because I'm a vampire that won't drink blood."

Professor Toad begins scrawling the history of the Academy of Six onto the board at the front and still I stare at the sharp angles of Saint's perfect features.

While I watch the vampire vacantly, large swooping letters magically drift across the board of their own accord:

In Eighteen Sixty-Six, six of the founding Prodigums joined forces after decades of what is now known as the Dark Genocide. Their efforts were successful in dethroning the reckless leader of the Dark Genocide once and for all. Lucian Morningstar, a powerful Prod...

"Miss Castillo, if you would please give our studies on the history of the Dark Genocide a rare moment of your time, the entire class would be appreciative." A mocking but monotone voice calls back to me.

My head snaps up and I'm met with those protruding eyes. "Yes, Mr. Toad."

His thin lips curl back from his crooked teeth. "It's *Professor Moore.*" His beady glare alone is writing up a detention slip as we speak.

"Right." I nod. Smile. Nod. Smile one more fucking time before he finally turns his insulted attention back to his lesson.

And then my gaze slips to Saint all over again.

I just can't believe how well he fakes it. He acts like he understands everything, like he has the entire world in his deadly palm.

He's just as lost as I am.

These terrible, frustrating, powerful men I surround myself with, are just as broken and confused as I am.

I wish I could say my endless questions have simmered some since first period.

They have not.

"So can you eat food?"

Saint sighs with exasperation. "Yes, I can eat food."

My barrage of questions doesn't stop. But really, what did he expect when he confessed the truth? That I'd just nod and say, "Oh, you poor dear."? I'm not his fucking grandmother. And I'm curious.

I need answers.

Like does he have his own blood? Does it pump through his veins? What's supporting that erection I saw when we first met?

These are all vital questions that need answers.

"Prove it." I shove my lunch tray in his direction, pointing at whatever concoction the lunch ladies brewed today in their cauldron. It looks like a strange mixture of oatmeal and beans with fatty chicken slices. I don't fucking know. "Take a bite *right now*. This stuff here, eat the bean porridge, Saint."

He shoves it across the table back in front of me. "Are you trying to poison me? God, woman, leave me alone. Phoenix, tell your girlfriend to leave me alone."

A weird feeling tingles through me at being called his girlfriend.

Irrational hormones that need to calm their ass down. That's what those feelings are.

At my side, Phoenix's lips twitch into the beginnings of a smile. I think he's amused by the whole conversation. I'm not quite sure how it happened, but by the time lunch came around, both Phoenix and Saint were waiting for me. Saint with a smile of greeting and Phoenix with an intense glare in his eyes, followed by a possessive hand slipping around my waist, where it's been ever since.

His fingers slip ever so slightly under the blazer, under my shirt and press into my warm skin. I wonder if that's all just for show or if he actually likes the feel of my skin against his.

It threatens to drive me to madness.

Is there a spell someone around here could bibbity-bobbity-boo on me to get these fucking hormones back on a steady track?

"No," Phoenix muses. "You're on your own, Saint." I swear I hear emotion in his voice.

"But you're a vampire and you need blood to survive,

so what do you drink?" I pin my attention back on the vampire seated across from me.

"Synthetic." As if he's proving a point to me, he waves around a can I'd assumed was some special hipster concoction Malek made him. The drink is fizzy and I can smell the poison from across the table.

"Junk food for vampires," Phoenix sneers distastefully at it.

So I'm not the only one who thinks so.

"Hey, synthetic blood has the same taste as feck blood, just without the added diabetes and possible diseases," he defends.

I don't think I've ever heard of a vampire who doesn't drink blood. Most vampires in this place are likely here because they crave it *too* much.

"Without the nutrients, too," I mumble, picking up my fork to toss the contents around.

I'm not going to touch this stuff and seeing it just makes me hungrier for real food. At this rate, they won't need to kill me for being Prodless, as I'll likely starve before that. So I play around with the food, creating Mr. Toad's double chin with a pile of brown beans.

"I'm what my family calls a vegetarian vampire." Saint crushes the can in his grasp.

I despair at the sight. I may not have my paints, but I could've made a tin sculpture with that thing. My fingers are craving art like my stomach craves my dad's cooking. It's an ache I can't ignore.

"Sounds like you jumped out of a Twilight novel." I

use the chicken fat stuff for Mr. Toad's eyes and a pack of sugar for his wisps of hair.

Phoenix's nails dig into my skin. It's not painful, and I think he's trying to hold himself from laughing. I sneak a peek at the sharp angle of his face. His red hair falls over his forehead just slightly, making him look a bit boyish despite his bulky frame. I reach out and push it away.

The simple brush of my fingers causes him to still, his eyes go that dangerous, demonic dark color I should fear, but don't. It's so easy to forget this is fake. With his arm wrapped around my waist and the three of us chatting like we're actually friends. Maybe, in a strange way, that's what we're becoming.

Friends.

I pull my hand away but he stops me by grabbing my wrist. It's held tensely there between us as we stare at one another. My mouth opens as I start to apologize but I never get the words out because a moment later, he's pressing his tongue to my fingertips in a way that's all too sensual, suggestive.

Fuck. How is this erotic? It shouldn't be. But my thighs quiver as he takes a finger into his mouth and sucks it deep. A tingling sensation starts at the tip of my finger and races through every single nerve ending before pulsing right through my clit and the entire feel of it pulls a rasping moan from my lips.

"Jesus Christ, you two, you're in the fucking cafeteria, for crying out loud."

I jolt, pulling my hand from Phoenix's grasp and turn

sharply as Malek appears, slamming his tray down next to Saint. The vampire makes room for him at our table, staring with that amused sparkle of mischief in his eyes like he's the devil pulling strings on his two favorite puppets.

Like he knows something fun is about to happen and he's eating it up.

Malek glares between the two of us, glasses sliding slightly down the ridge of his nose.

Holy fucking gods in heaven, is he good looking. He's all scruff along that prominent jawline, his long hair pushed back into a short ponytail. He's perfectly put together and carrying, of all things, a book in one hand.

The werewolf fanfic girl in me squeals into a puddle of desire.

Pounding energy spreads slow and torturously through me. I think the incubus can literally smell the shift in my emotions, because he emanates a low warning growl and tugs me closer, the gesture possessive.

Like he owns me.

The line between fake boyfriend and jealous real boyfriend is... gone. It's completely gone, I think.

I don't understand it at all.

And a part of me, can't help but test him just to see what's real between us.

"You look good today," I compliment Malek as he takes his seat.

His eyes slash over me, assessing damage, and there's something equally possessive about his stare that I can't help but to relish in. I feel like a total Prod tease, but I can't bring myself to care when three deadly Prods of Academy of Six are staring at me like I'm the last glass of cold water in the desert they've been traveling through for days.

Malek looks back up to me, and somehow I can tell he's remembering the night before. Maybe because I'm remembering it, recalling the feel of his arms wrapping around me, the comforting lilt of his singing voice bringing me back from the darkness.

"So do you." He smiles and my panties nearly melt to the floor.

They're academy panties so I don't really need the cheap material, anyway.

"What do you want, mutt?" Phoenix asks flatly.

Too much testosterone threatens to suffocate me.

Malek dismisses my fake boyfriend with half a glance. It's like he gives no fucks what he has to say and directs all the attention of his heated gaze to me. "I brought you something."

My body straightens and I smile at the prospect of a gift. My fingers grasp the book he passes my way. It's binding is leather, the pages frail and wrinkled. It's certainly not new. The paper smells crisp and worn, like an old library that holds the secrets of adventures. I open it and turn the delicate pages. The inside is scrawled in bold ink and detailed pictures of demons and angels, God's horsemen, of creatures so grotesque it hurts to look at them. They move across the page in swirling ink like art themselves as they depict stories and facts. History come to life on the thinnest parchment within the oldest bindings known to man.

It's beautiful.

"It's a book about the rare Prods. I thought it might help you figure out what you are."

Be still, my little Prodless heart.

He cares. Malek really does care about me. Whatever happened last night, and the images are a bit blurred, all I know is that I fainted into darkness just as the memories started to surface, just as they brushed across my fingertips, something changed between us.

This is friendship. *Real* friendship, not fake. I can feel the difference.

And that's care in his gaze. Even when he pulled away last night and encased himself in a shell, he cared enough to find me this book, something that would help me control the beast inside, defend myself, and likely not get killed by the academy.

Emotion threatens to close tightly within my throat.

"Thanks," I whisper, closing the pages and hugging it close to my chest. This gift, it's perfect. Malek is perfect in a way that somehow is completely endearing.

He gifts me with a lopsided smile that's filled with warmth that I imagine tastes like home and safety and everything in between.

"That all, Kibbles?" Phoenix's low voice is a testing sound. "You can fuck off now."

Malek slashes a glare at Phoenix but he doesn't

linger. The precarious moment that lay between us is broken the moment my fake boyfriend speaks. Malek's walls rebuild as quickly as they quietly fell down and, a moment later, he's standing, pulling his tray with him. "See you in gym."

And then he's gone.

My head turns so slowly to the man still holding me against his warm side.

"God, you're such a dick." I pick up my fork, tearing it through my temporary food masterpiece. I jerk from him so his hand falls away from my skin. I hate to admit that I miss his touch, that I crave it the way beautiful wolves miss the moonlight.

Phoenix Rutherford is blatantly bad for me, and I still want him.

"He was eye fucking you, in case you didn't notice, *baby*." He sounds jealous now.

Saint passes a glance at his best friend, a smirk tilting his lips, but he doesn't comment.

"So what?" My shoulders pull up in a shrug that's so tense, I have to force them back down.

"So, you were eye fucking him back," he says coldly, wild darkness eating away at the pretty green in his gaze. It's like ink running across a page. The black color starts from his pupils, consumes the irises and doesn't stop until it's darkening the thin veins beneath his eyes.

Saint's attention darts back and forth between us, a smile widening his mouth like he's watching the best fucking play he's ever seen. Phoenix is making a scene.

As if it matters to him one way or another who I eye fuck. He hates me.

And we're nothing. We're a fake relationship that's so fragile it can't even make it two full days.

"So *what*?" I ask so slowly, so pointedly.

Out of the corner of my eye I see Phoenix's jaw tighten as his white teeth grind together, like he's barely holding in the rage he wants to unleash. The veins around his eyes start to pulse and bulge now. If I didn't know any better, I'd say the soulless incubus feels something.

"So, my girlfriend won't be eye fucking a mutt right in front of me."

"Maybe not behind you either, right?" Saint suggests but his amused words go unheard.

I sigh and push the tray away. I've suddenly lost my appetite for food art. "I'm not yours, Nubbie."

"Nubbie?" the demon echoes incredulously.

Saint bursts out laughing, a crackling lingering sound, but still goes ignored.

I cross my arms over my chest when I face Phoenix. His gaze strays to the tightness of the shirt against my chest that the parted lapels of the blazer reveal. He can look all he wants. Boy is getting no action except in his incubus dreams if he continues to act like a piece of shit.

And honestly, I'm going to start avoiding his sleep schedule because he cannot be trusted.

"Malek is nice. He's my friend, and you can't tell me not to have friends when you don't even like me."

Phoenix snorts, and I know he's holding emotions in, pushing it down deep in his obnoxiously broad chest but it just pulses back up in every black throb of his veins and dilation of his pupils.

"Friends don't get wet for other friends." He leans closer between our chairs so our chests are pressed against each other. One hand goes to my bare thigh and skims up to the hem of my skirt, lifting... "I could touch your pussy right now and feel how wet you are for that mutt."

I want to jerk away from the crudeness of his words, I want to push his roaming fingers away from me, but they're drifting higher and higher, and a part of me wants him to touch where he promises, to feel his fingers against my folds, but a bigger part of me can't let this challenge go unanswered.

My thighs part dauntingly.

"And you care, why? Don't forget..." I drop my voice to a whisper, lift my leg just so his fingers fall even closer to my center. It's a dare and a threat rolled together. "This relationship is *fake*."

My words seem to cut through him. He yanks his hand back as if my body branded him. I hope it fucking did. I hope he feels my touch at his fingertips and aches for the feel of my skin until his cock explodes from need like it should have when he stupidly downed a pallet of Viagra in an attempt to fucking feel something. I want him to walk away from me knowing he can't have me, can't control me, no matter what deal we strike or how hard we pretend.

I want him to want me and not be able to do a fucking thing about it.

Phoenix stands stiffly, impatiently. His eyes are packed with hatred, his nostrils flaring. He's unreadable. But I don't need to read him to know that I've won.

"See you in gym," he growls and whirls away.

I watch him go with a sad smile on my face.

"You're a cruel, cruel woman, Izara Castillo," Saint whistles appreciatively.

I have to be in this place where niceties scarcely exist and cruelty is power and punishment. I'll embrace it in all its savage, darkened form.

If only to survive this fucking joke of a school.

As well as my friends.

FOURTEEN

Saint

The anger in his eyes is hard to look at. You'd think I'd be used to it by now. I've seen it there since we were kids.

And I hate it now as much as I ever did then. He was always the one thing that made me feel steady, like I wasn't falling when my father beat me an inch from my life or kicked me out in the dead of night to really straighten me out.

Phoenix was always there. And that's why I'll always be there for him. Even if he fucks up day in and day out.

The bedroom door closes behind me and I just stare at him as he glares up at the rotting boards of his bunk. He ran right here like I knew he would.

Those fancy Academy of Six ankle bracelets don't exactly give him too many hiding spot options. Or maybe I just know the incubus too well, knew he'd come here to mope and rage, get lost in the confusion of his own lack of feelings after that mess with Izzy.

A sigh pushes from my lungs just looking at him.

It isn't that he hates Izzy. He just... he hates everyone.

She doesn't stand a fucking chance. But I hope she tries.

Fuck, I hope they both try, for his sake.

My quiet steps lead me to him but his gaze refuses to meet mine even as I settle at the edge of his mattress. My palms splay low, sliding down the hard planes of his abs, stopping right at the line of his dark briefs peeking out above his jeans. Sweat dampens his skin and I'm surprised he isn't naked in this hellhole.

"I know she can help you. And you can help her. If you just calm down," I whisper, my teeth extending just from feeling his warm skin against mine, it's hard to swallow when I touch him. Hard to form basic thoughts even.

"I am calm." The growl of his words shouldn't make me instantly hard, but I just fucking can't help it.

"That's not calm." As I lean forward, my head dips, my lips grazing his jaw line, wishing like hell the brooding man had a pulse.

If he had a pulse, I'd know how he felt about me.

But he doesn't. And I don't.

We're both a mess.

"This is calm." When my teeth move ever so lightly across his perfect skin, the tension falls from his shoulders, the only indication he's ever enjoyed what we are together.

My fingers slip lower and his silence is a daring thing. There's no groans or gasps, there's no lust within Phoenix at all, but he's always fucking *hard*.

That constant quiet fucking kills me. His emptiness slices up my heart, hurting me as much as it hurts him.

My mouth trails lower just as my hand does, palming his thick outline over his jeans.

Whatever god is out there, he's a cruel fuck for giving Phoenix a cock this big, but never letting him enjoy it.

A total waste.

My head dips lower, my kisses and words getting lost in his body. "I can calm you."

A strong hand grips the side of my neck and with two sudden steps he lifts me and pins me with a hard clash against the metal bunk bed across from his. Blazing eyes search mine, aggression radiating off him in a way that should. Not. Turn. Me. On.

"If you want me calm, then let me do what I'm supposed to fucking do." He bites the words out like a threat but his chest melds to mine.

My lips brush over his.

"Then fuck me," I challenge with a slow flicking kiss.

And it's a dirty fucking challenge that I know he loves. He loves sex even if he can't feel it.

If I had to guess, I'd say he's envious of what he makes others feel. And fuck is he good at making me feel every fucking inch of him.

He leans closer with a pureness in his emerald eyes, his lips pressing to mine with surprising gentleness. Long fingers slide beneath my jeans just as his tongue slides perfectly over mine. He takes his time with dedicated slowness, stroking down my cock, inch by inch, before bringing the heel of his palm right across my head and making me groan into his claiming mouth.

The squeal of the hinges is the only sound and even that telling noise isn't enough to make me pull away from the way he's sucking my lower lip.

"Um..." Her quiet voice hums right into me, making my dick pulse in Phoenix's hand just from the soft sound of it. I pull back, but we never untangle ourselves. I'm still grasping his neck and he's still...he's still grasping my cock. "I—I really need my notes." Izzy's dark lashes flutter closed, heat flushing across her pretty face the longer she stands awkwardly in the doorway, not daring to cross the two of us in the middle of the room.

The smirk pulling at my lips only grows the longer her uncomfortable situation drags out.

Finally, I shift out from beneath Phoenix's big body, his frustrated sigh growling right out of him as he releases me.

The black binder near her bed catches my attention and I bring it to the poor girl still standing with her eyes closed.

Is she humiliated or turned on?

With her small body inches from mine, thoughts of how perfect she'd fit pressed right between Phoenix and I fill my head. I push the binder into her hands with so much slowness my fingertips caress each curve of her knuckles.

"Anything else?" I ask with a —hopeful—hinting smile.

She shakes her head hard. But then her big amber eyes open, looking up at me with the strangest, confusion shining there.

"I—I didn't realize you two were—"

The single step I take closer to her, eliminating any suggestion of space, cuts her words away in her throat, her pulse drilling wildly there.

My lips brush there at the base of her neck, tasting her apprehension and loving the way her heartbeat kisses my lips.

The warmth of her body sends old memories of how hot blood used to taste along my tongue.

Once upon a time.

"We're not," I whisper, lingering, waiting and watching and hoping like fuck she'll steal my confidence and come inside like we both know she wants to.

She's an enigma. Sometimes she's quiet and reserved. And sometimes she forces her assertiveness to shine out to hide how weak she is in this place without a dependable Prod within her to protect her.

"Don't be late, Feck. Wouldn't want another night of isolation," Phoenix taunts coldly from just behind me, all but pissing over my fantasies.

My jaw clenches so hard I hear teeth crack just slightly.

Those lashes flutter as if she's washing away a crazy thought in that pretty mind of hers.

And then she turns and walks away.

Why is he like this? Why does he hate everyone?

Including me.

My fingers dig into the wooden doorframe, letting it splinter down the center beneath my anger.

And then I walk away, too.

"Where are you going?" His voice crawls down the dark hall after me.

I don't have the control to face him and not walk right back into him.

If I look at him, if I meet those tortured green eyes, I'll be sucked in all over again.

And I'm not doing that. Not today.

"I'm going to find your feck. You promised to be there for her during gym. She needs someone there."

His curses whisper down the corridor to me for several seconds.

Then his steady footfalls are following after me. The smallest smile tilts my lips.

He cares. He cares about me and he cares about her. He just doesn't know it.

FIFTEEN

Izara

Gym: Welcome to Hell.

Enjoy the under-boob sweat, embrace your ass jiggles with every lap you run, and by all means, try not to cry too much as you cling to the bottom of a hanging rope and attempt to understand what the fuck this is preparing you for in life.

I wonder if the devil himself is the coach inside this quaint little gymnasium.

I stand before the building and I don't want to go in. Cardio? Weights? This academy is trying to kill me. If I promise to be a good little Prod and not murder any more boyfriends, will they let me skip?

Probably not.

Striding footsteps sound behind me and I don't know how I know, but I know it's Saint. He just has that air about him. He walks like someone who doesn't look at price tags when he shops, someone who doesn't pay attention to the pump when he gets fuel, someone who just uses whatever credit card his careless fingers land on.

That's what his pretentious footsteps sound like, if you can believe it.

And I don't want to face him or any of his Phoenix excuses right now. I can't be friends with Malek, but Phoenix can give his best friend a hand job? What kind of shit is that? It's a roommate mess where I live. Someone please fucking explain the rules and regulations of fake relationships because we are hopeless.

I rush forward even as Saint calls my name.

Steeling myself for the worst, I push open the wide double doors of the building and step inside.

And it's like being dropped face first into the middle of a Tolkien battle.

Fire flies past me, almost singeing my eyebrows. Winged Prods push themselves off high rafter beams near the ceiling and soar, only to collide in mid-air. Faerie like girls with sharp features make vines grow in a corner that twist up like corded ropes only to climb up them at rapid speeds moments later. Sparks rain down from the ceiling from a flying creature I can't even see among the flames. Shifters snarl mid change as they wrestle on soft blue mats, tearing through flesh with tooth and claw.

Sure, there are some dusty treadmills in the corner. And yeah, I think that centaur is doing a basic horse pushup, but the bizarre definitely outweighs the ordinary here.

This is gym?

It's a battle of beasts everywhere I turn and I don't know quite where to look first. At the feathery hawk wings of a female as she engages in a fight, looking like a Valkyrie of legends, or at the demon and fae training with gauze around their hands like boxing gloves.

"You must be Izara Castillo."

I startle when a man suddenly appears before me. It takes me a moment to tear my gaze away from the fray and notice he's holding a hand out to me.

I look at it suspiciously, knowing this must be some trick. No one is nice at this school, so why is he?

Reluctantly, I shake his hand and pull it away just as quickly. Then I look up at his face and my heart stops cold in my chest.

Fuck, he's the most alluring man I've ever seen. He's made of beauty that surpasses that of an incubus, a form stronger than a wolf's, but it's his eyes that draw me in.

Bicolored and glowing, one is pure gold. Not honey, but actual gold, glittering with shining specks. The other is black. I'm not sure which eye to look, the demonic one or the angelic one, for there's no doubt in my mind that that's what this man is. He's a mix of both things, like heaven and hell somehow collided into an explosion that molded this perfect person.

And I'm staring stupidly at the older man.

"That's me." The way my words fall vacantly from my lips is the opposite of his assured charm.

He smiles dazzlingly. "I'm Professor Shade."

Professor. This stunning man is a teacher at this establishment? He doesn't look the part. He's a far cry from Mr. Toad. His shining black hair with one lone strip of white at the front is slicked back. He looks the very definition of a professional, even wearing a gray pants suit.

His bicolored gaze roams over me, not lewdly, or judgingly, but assessing like a scientist studying a peculiar specimen under a microscope. When those eyes flick back to my face, his smile widens.

"Let me guess... fae?"

Why the fuck does everyone keep saying that?

"No," I grind out tightly. "My Prod is playing hide and seek at the moment."

His expression doesn't change. There's no pity. Nothing. I almost feel like a normal student and not a feck.

"Never fear, we'll discover what your Prod is together. That's the purpose of this class, to push your body to the limit in an attempt to bring out your Prod in a safe, controlled environment." He turns and I take it as a command to follow.

The doors bang shut behind me and I glance back just in time to meet deep green eyes that burn across my features. So much for Phoenix's unwavering protection.

He said he'd be here. He wasn't, *and* he's late.

I guess Saint's dick must have weighed him down.

I hope isolation is a kick in his balls. Not that I'm too worried about him or his balls at the moment. My shoulders stiffen and I follow Profesor Shade.

We weave our way through the destructive bodies of

clashing Prods. He's confident in his stride, meanwhile I try not to get pelted with acid spit from nearby lizard creatures.

"Here you'll learn to bring out the basest of your beast's instincts. Training will force it out of you, and I will teach you control."

We step off the mats and walk down into a hallway. There's a small office here, and two separate doors.

"Locker rooms and showers," he indicates with a gesture of his hand. He leads me into his office where he grabs a small key and passes it to me. "For your locker. You'll find your uniform there already."

Of course it is. Uniforms are Academy of Six's number one priority.

My hand wraps around the key, the cold sharpness of it digging into my palm.

"I'm not going to lie to you, Izara," the Professor says. His tone is soft but firm, his eyes hard and full of determination. "For a girl with an unknown Prod, this class will be hell. You will be pushed and beaten. It's kill or be killed, but do as I say and by the end of the year, your Prod will show itself and you'll be reformed in no time."

I wonder if he knows what I've done. If he knows I've killed. He knew my name, he must have read my file, even if he feigned obliviousness by calling me a fae. Being Prodless is no easy thing, that's been made clear. We are discarded, discriminated. But he looks like he genuinely wants to help me.

I don't know if I should be wary or relieved.

"They say there's no hope for the Prodless," I mutter sarcastically.

Those features of his soften. Maybe he does care.

"I believe there is. You just need that extra push and I intend to help you along the way. But you have to listen to me. Trust me. Can you do that?"

"Why would you go out of your way to help a Prodless?" I can't help the slip of words. "Most teachers seem to hate us."

Vehemence flares in his multicolored eyes. He leans back against his wooden desk, crossing one ankle over the other, arms firmly against his chest.

"You'll find, Izara, that I am not most teachers." He looks away and I notice the tightening of his sharp jaw. When he looks back, there's sadness in his eyes. "My child was considered a Prodless."

This captures my attention. I lean forward, my whole body nearly trembling with curiosity.

"What happened?"

He pushes himself off the desk and walks to the door.

His short, clipped words linger in the room until it crawls up my skin and into my chest with the weight of his expression alone.

"He died."

I try not to dwell on his words as I change into a blue and

red shirt and shorts, but they resonate through my mind like a song on repeat.

He died.

I pull my hair back into a ponytail and go out to join the others.

He died.

These are my only options in a future that's set in stone. Control myself or die.

And I don't want to die.

All the Prods gather around Professor Shade.

Malek's dark eyes meet mine and he takes quiet steps until he's at my side, his warm shoulder lightly brushing mine in a dominating stance.

Phoenix doesn't look my way, gaze intently held straight ahead.

"Welcome to hell, Prods." The Professor's hands clasp behind his lower back, walking a line back and forth like a military drill sergeant. "Let's talk semester final exams."

A cacophony of groans ring out.

"We *just* started school," someone complains.

Professor Shade ignores it. "The final exam will consist of one thing and one thing only: *winning*." A hush falls over us all. He definitely has our attention. "You will be separated into teams and pitted against each other. You each will have two goals: protect your flag, and capture the opposing team's flag."

Excited murmurs shudder like a wave through the crowd of students.

This, this sounds like the gym I expected. If he mentions the words touch football or scrimmage after this, I'm gone.

"The rules are simple. You will fight, you will use your magic and unleash your Prods. You will do this to disarm, not to maim or kill. Do so and you are disqualified and will be expelled. Do *nothing* and you are disqualified and will be expelled. This activity is mandatory, any refusal to cooperate, you will be disqualified and expelled."

I am so fucked. Or should I say expelled.

"The next few weeks we will train to prepare you for the exam. You will push your bodies and learn the control you lack. I suggest you take it seriously."

His alluring gaze shifts over each of us individually. Then without another word, he separates us into groups.

Surprise, fucking surprise, I'm with Phoenix, Malek, Saint, Syko and a poor faerie girl with resting bitch face who has absolutely no idea what kind of Prod drama she's signed up for with us.

It's a pattern I notice. He puts together winged creature, demon, shifter, vampire, fae, and a Prodless in every group. Sometimes warlocks and witches get thrown into the mix, but for the most part, the class seems lacking of them.

I guess he thinks we'll be each other's strengths and make up for each other's weaknesses.

And maybe we will.

If we don't kill each other first.

SIXTEEN

Syko

Karlyn's back hits my bunk just as a large man falls on top of her, a nasty scar slicing right across his face from one brow, across his nose, and down to his lip. His thrusts against her are so hard, I'm sure he's going to break the faerie's hips before he ever gets to fuck her.

It's been three weeks. Three weeks, and we go through this every single fucking week.

My gaze flashes to my sister in an instant and the color in her eyes flickers like a bad signal just before a storm.

Shit.

"Karlyn. I think... I think we discussed visitors. Yeah, we definitely had an agreement." I stand from my bed just as Scarface pushes down Karlyn's pink panties as if I never even fucking spoke.

I try a different approach. "You know you're like the

third guy she's fucked this week, right?" My statement is followed by an uncaring silence and frantic gasping breaths. "Wouldn't be a big deal, but it's only Monday afternoon, you know?" I shrug, my attention slipping back to my little sister, who's whole body is now flickering dangerously in and out of focus, not just her eyes.

Shit.

I slip past them as a sharp and fucking terrifying shriek claws up the fae's throat as Scarface thrusts in. She's part banshee, I think. Her orgasms sound like a pissed off security alarm. And not in a good way.

The door slides open, banging into the guy's shoulder, but he just keeps on going. My eyes roll hard and I nod for Kayos to follow. The two of us trail out into the quiet hall and I pull the door shut behind us.

Being out here soothes the building storm inside her. I see the discreet breaths she's taking, the ones we learned were calming from watching all those yoga videos together. I've looked for so many ways to keep her anger at bay. For her own safety, as well as everyone else's.

"We got an hour to kill it looks like." I stretch my arms over my head, cupping my hands to the back of my neck in a casual stance.

"I give him four minutes, tops," Kayos says like the total smartass that she is.

She makes me so proud some days.

Quiet footsteps trail up the hall and the sway of her hips alone in that short khaki skirt tells me exactly who it is.

"Don't embarrass us this time." The warning hiss from my sister goes unheard.

Izara's limping, her face scrunching up as if with every step she takes her muscles are screeching in violent protest.

"You look like you've been through hell." The way my hands sink into my pockets is mostly to make sure I don't do something stupid.

Like shove my neighbor up against the wall and see if I can get her to say all the dirty things I know she bites back when she looks at me.

I could force the truth out of her. But... I've learned my lesson from using my abilities for all the wrong reasons.

I think...

"Not hell. Just gym." Her shoulders sag and she turns the knob of her dorm door without another word.

She's just about to shut the door when she peers up and finds us still standing aimlessly in the middle of the dark hall. Like lost puppies without an owner, I'm sure that's what she sees.

"What are you doing?" She looks from me to Kayos.

"Our roommate is in the middle of another disappointing four minutes of her life," Kayos tells her flatly.

"What?" Her narrow gaze just highlights the warm flecks of gold in the dark brown of her irises. Just the color of her eyes brings enough warmth and light through the wisps of shadows in these halls.

"Karlyn is entertaining." I add, head nodding, hands still safely shoved into my khakis.

A banshee cry screeches suddenly through the silence and Izara's dark sculpted brow arches just subtly.

Life is just fucking perfect here.

"Um... you guys want to come in for a bit?"

"Fuck, please," I blurt.

The smallest smile pulls at her lips and the way her mouth reveals that perfect dimple in her left cheek causes my heart to applaud every part of her beauty.

"Don't embarrass us," Kayos hisses as we slip inside.

I pass the little girl a glare but to be honest, no threatening look I give her could ever be as terrifying as what she hides inside herself.

I don't even know why I try.

"You're in Interdimensional Travels, right? I saw you two sitting toward the back today." She sits cross-legged on a lower bunk, her skirt barely covering between her smooth thighs.

I linger in the middle of the small room, not wanting to invade her space any more than I already am.

"I am. Are you excited to be visiting *the void of which your heart desires?*" I mimic Professor Zent's ominous tone, and I'm rewarded with another of her soft smiles that almost touches her eyes.

She makes me think she doesn't have a lot of happiness in her life.

"I tried, but my void is apparently *too* void." Her lips pull down and it's enough to make me take a seat at her side, pulling her papers from her hands before she can fall deeper into that frown.

Izara Castillo is strong. Strong but...careful. A little terrified of herself in a way.

And that's what's holding her back from *the void*.

I force myself to look away from her and I peer up for only a second to find Kayos pawing through a dresser drawer in the closet. She holds up a pair of black boxers and makes a promptly disgusted face before tossing them to the side and to keep searching.

"It's easier if you've been there. You don't know where you're from though, so you don't have too many places you could go." I scan her pages of notes.

She's trying. She's got every word that old hack has ever said jotted down here. But it's all for nothing if she doesn't have a foundation to work from and if she doesn't trust herself.

"My father adopted me when I was just a baby." Her tone is just shy of a whisper. I lean into the pretty sound of it. "He's a warlock, but he's put distance between the supernatural society and himself. I don't really know a lot about supernaturals in general. It feels—I feel like I already failed and I haven't even started yet."

I don't know why she confesses this to me, but I'm glad she does. My hand slips over to hers, but she has a lifeless touch as my fingers brush back and forth over the small curves of her knuckles. "Failure is only monumental if you build it up before it falls." The quote is something I've heard so many damn times in my life.

I've just never said it out loud to anyone before.

"Wow," her brows lift and fuck if I don't love the way she's looking at me right now.

I wonder if my grandpa has any other inspirational quotes I could steal to get laid?

"My grandpa always said that. Mostly to me. Kayos is too smart to need any advice from anyone."

Her smile tilts, and she passes a look to the little girl who's currently leafing through a small notebook.

"Your drawings are overemotional," my sister says vacantly.

"Kayos. Fuck. Stop." I nearly stand to pull her evading search away before any illusion of privacy is completely destroyed. Izzy tugs me back down at her side with a gentle squeeze of my hand though.

"No. She's—She's right. Art is entirely overemotional."

"It means your work is good," Kayos murmurs as she continues flipping page after mysterious page.

"Can I look?" I tilt my head to get a better view of the ink lined pages but Izzy dips her head into my line of sight.

"No. *Angel*, you cannot look." Her taunting nickname burns so warmly in my chest, I can't help but glare at her.

"What the fuck! Kayos got to see." I'm almost stomping my foot with a wide smile, but she shoves me back when I try to make a lunge for it.

I wrestle her small hands away and my heartbeat

purrs to life with every touch of her skin brushing mine. So I do it again. I lunge, she shoves, I twist, and she grips both wrists. And then with those slender fingers sliding over my pecs, she pushes me down entirely against the thin mattress and covers my body with her soft curves. Smooth thighs lock around my stomach, my shirt shoved up high and granting me the full effect of her heat that's pressed firmly against my abs.

Our smiles shine, her breath mixing with mine until all I fucking breathe is her happiness. She releases me slowly but never pulls back. I can't help but settle my free hands on the curve of those hips I watch too frequently.

The moment I touch her there, logic falls into her warm honey eyes.

Shit.

"Sorry." The whisper is a breath of a word as she slides off of my hard body and stands, smoothing her skirt down and finding her buttons are undone at the bottom of her shirt.

The door crawls open with a tiny cry and the creep that paws all over her at lunch fills the doorway with his broad shoulders.

His green gaze shifts from me lying on Izzy's bed to his roommate who's re-buttoning her shirt at my side.

Double shit.

"What the fuck are you doing over here, Bird Boy?"

His voice is all suspicion and hard anger. Because it's totally normal for me to have sex and fuck at Izara in front of my kid sister. Of course, logic won't work on this brute of a demon.

He has the gaze of someone who kills firsts and asks questions *never*.

"Okay. Can we at least remember that I'm a fucking nephilim, not an angel, not a bird, *a nephilim?*"

In three big steps he's in my face and my body weight falls away as he lifts me right off the damn bunk. He hauls me up with rage shaking through him and my wings fling out in less than a second. Ethereal light shines across his scowling features the moment my wings extend. The force and quickness in which I bring them out physically hurts. I feel the shirt at my back rip, the blood coating every feather and sliding down the length of my back. The length of my wings nearly touches one side of the wall and the other, but there's enough space in here for me to push them in powerful strokes.

And then it's him that's being lifted by me.

With big shifting moves of my wings I keep him there several feet off the ground.

"My name's Syko. What's yours?" I ask, my hand slipping between us as he clutches my shoulders harder to keep from falling.

"Fucking bird shifters."

"*Nephilim.* I'm born of literal heavenly powers. Please, take notice." My hands lift from my sides as he lets go, giving a growl before falling to his knees on the floor. I finally drop on the heels of my shoes and stride to the door where Kayos waits with an aloof look on her tired face.

"I asked you not to embarrass us," she mumbles as we walk into the safety of the hall.

I shake my head at her and turn back for a single second to see the surprised look in Izzy's eyes.

"Thanks for entertaining us." My wink makes her smile widen until the little dimple in her cheek shows, exploding gratifying happiness throughout my chest with the sight of it.

"Bye, Kayos," Izzy says sweetly.

Kayos gives a little wave. "I like her. Work harder to show her you have more potential than the demon." My sister doesn't even look at me, but her bluntly demeaning words remind me too much of my grandpa.

Kayos approves of her. Kayos doesn't approve of anyone.

Fuck, I like Izara even more now.

SEVENTEEN

Izara

I've made it months here. Four to be exact. Things have settled, a routine has fallen into play in my life just as it did in the human world.

The thing is, I'm still Prodless.

Everything's different. But exactly the fucking same.

"Pair up, my Prods," Professor Zent instructs in the grumbling tone of his, like a grandfather clock literally coming to life.

Phoenix and Saint sit side by side at a table. Syko glances at me but stays at his table with his sister. And just as I have for months, I sit with Malek. He's my safe place really. There's nothing but patience in him no matter how many times everyone around us dissolves away with the magic of their Prods and we sit glued to this damn classroom like I'll never fucking leave.

Anxiety thrums through my chest as everyone gets

into position for the lesson, but the one thing that calms me is having Malek. He's gentle, even his rumbling tone is a gentle sound. His touch, god, his touch is gentle.

He smiles, that dark beard and dark eyes doing so much good for my soul.

His beard is good for my soul. I don't know how to explain it but that's what power men's beards have. It's a warm and fuzzy sort of comfort that just tells me he can take care of me. He can go out and chop down an entire forest to build me a castle, a carriage, and my own fucking happily ever after.

Beards create happily ever afters for women with a single smile.

Total fucking calm.

"Miss Castillo you'll be working with Mr. Rutherford this morning. I've never had a failure before in my class and I refuse to start with you. Mr. Von Hunter swap seats." A wave of wrinkles scrunch over his face as Professor Zent gives me a waiting look, ripping away my security blanket and tossing me to the wolves... Or should I say ripping me away from my wolf and tossing me to the demon.

The air never hits my lungs even as I look across the aisle and meet Phoenix's expressionless emerald gaze. Saint stands so quickly it's suspicious. It's literally the first time I've ever seen him do as he's told without flipping the teacher the middle finger as he goes.

He's such a perfect student he pulls out his chair for me as I begrudgingly wander over to my new partner.

"Don't be an ass," Saint growls to his friend under his breath as he passes him.

"I'll just be myself," Phoenix shrugs lightly.

"Right... don't be yourself either." Saint arches a brow at him and the dead look in Phoenix's eyes makes me wonder why Saint even tries.

The two of them give me a headache just listening to them. Saint tries too hard for the both of them and Phoenix... I don't know. Sometimes we're fake friends, sometimes we're fake dating, and sometimes... we're just fake.

"Do you travel every time, or is it hard for you?" I ask with a shaking, nervous tone giving me away.

His fiery hair almost touches his lashes as he looks at me, meeting my eyes with an almost pathetic look. "Zent put you with me because I travel *every time*."

Wow, brag much?

"Well, it takes two, a controller and a traveller, so... be prepared for a boring forty minutes or—"

The dim fluorescent lights burn away from my vision, transforming into a long mysterious hall constructed entirely of fire. My words fizzle away with the flickering sound of the darkened flames as my feet stumble over dirt.

"What. The. Fuck." I stand mindlessly in the center of it all.

The flames rise from pits of darkness on either side of us. The violent flicking tendrils press around us like arms that want to reach out, grab me, and drag me under. The heat is almost suffocating, and I feel the smoke press into my lungs, feel the sweat bead on my forehead, and slide in rivulets down my face.

"I'm not a hold-your-hand and baby you type of controller like your pet Malek. So..." He gestures around to all of this. "Why did you pick the center ring of hell?"

"I didn't pick this place. You're the demon, this is clearly your place."

"I'm the controller, you're the traveller. I'm good, but I'm not good enough to be the controller of time and space as well as the fucking navigator. Jesus, women really are shit with directions."

Aaannnd I hate him again.

His bulking arm brushes mine, the smooth skin of his forearm dragging my attention to just how close he's now hovering nearly right over me.

"Can you not be an asshole for, oh I don't know, the next forty minutes we're stuck in hell together?"

His smile is cruel when he turns to me with a look I've seen too many times to really trust him. Big hands push down my hips and he pulls me close.

"How do I know this isn't your way of just trying to get me alone for a bit?"

"If I wanted to get you alone, I'd stop avoiding your sleep schedule, asshole."

Confusion tenses his brows and he takes a step back from me.

"You've been avoiding my sleep schedule? I gave you orgasmic bliss and now you're sleep ghosting me?"

"You gave me a wet dream, let's call it what it was." My hands press to my hips.

"It was real. It was the only thing that's been real since I met you."

"It was hardly real."

"It *was* real," he nearly yells.

I get right back in his face, his gaze dropping to my mouth as I slowly say, "Your cock wasn't real. The sex wasn't real. We're not real, Phoenix."

He never flinches from my harsh words, but he does skim his lips slowly over mine like a punishment. And I melt. With hellacious heat all around me, I melt into the feel of his tongue stroking just lightly over mine.

"What about when you let your guard down and you let me kiss you like you want me? Is that real?"

The stumbling of my heart is a weak emotion that I won't allow to show on my face.

"If anyone else were here with me, they'd be asking me what monster lives inside me for me to bring us here to the center ring of hell. And you're so unbelievably selfish all you can ask is why I don't always show you how much I hate you."

"You mean Malek. If *Malek* were here he'd be asking you all the important things, right? Because he's so fucking in control of his emotions. And I don't have a clue what they even are." Big green eyes stare down on me with the smallest hint of his real feelings.

Sometimes I think I make this powerful, soulless man feels things he doesn't understand.

And sometimes, I think he's just a cruel jerk.

Right now, he's so raw and open, I know he feels more than he's showing. More than he's used to.

My shoes arch against the dirt and, on the tips of my toes, I press my lips to his, slowly tasting all the sad words he just confessed to me.

It's a small confession but one that I can tell is monumental for him.

"Thank you for bringing me here," I whisper to him, my fingers pushing through his thick hair as he touches his mouth to mine in a slow, drawn out brush of affection.

His eyes stay closed, and he holds me to him, his fingers digging into my skin, the heat of the flames licking my skin but I can't seem to pull away from him.

"Honestly, this place scares the shit out of me and I hate that *you* brought *us* here." He never pulls back from the slow work of our mouths despite his confusing words slipping between us.

I can't help but smirk at him even as countless questions about my Prod circle my mind over and over again.

"You're scared of me, huh?" His mouth drops lower and his tongue flicks slow nipping kisses down the side of my neck as if he thinks he might really have a chance at fucking me in the center ring of hell.

Nothing sets the mood like the smell of burnt hair and frying fat.

"You have no idea how terrifying you really are, Iz." His teeth rake a sensual drag of his sharp teeth just beneath my ear.

... Can we have sex in hell?

There's got to be a room for that here. I mean... it's hell so... sit my ass in the VIP section and I'm sure soon enough the devil himself will be stroking my hair and telling me I'm pretty.

"We need to get the fuck out of here before the ass proteges find us."

That gets my attention.

"I'm sorry the what?"

"Ass proteges. *Ass trolls.* They're sort of like pledges for frat houses. An older, wiser demon instructs them on the best way to literally torment someone from the asshole in."

What the literal hell?

"That's... incredibly detailed and informative. Thank you, Phoenix."

He gives an *anytime, anytime* kind of nod that does nothing for the tight disgusted way my stomach's twisting from his overly descriptive explanation.

"Yeah, let's get the fuck out of here before the asshole proteges show up," I say with a nod.

"Ass. *Ass proteges.*"

"Just stop saying it. Please."

A small shrug lifts his shoulder and then the flickering flames wash away. And terrible, harsh fluorescent lighting looms over us from overhead.

Ah. The first hell I ever loved: Academy of Six.

I fucking did it.

I traveled through dimensions. And time and space

and whatever the fuck else this old ass warlock is always rambling about.

I did it. I'm not a Prodless failure!

"Miss Castillo. Congratulations," Professor Zent murmurs, slashing little red lines across papers on his desk, not glancing up at me with his less than excited congrats he just gave. He does, however, pull a worn golden timepiece from the pocket of his velvet suit jacket. "It only took you eleven hours and six minutes." He smacks his lips patronizingly.

"Eleven hours?" I blurt out, the pride in me washing away into a pathetic puddle of disappointment.

"And six minutes," Phoenix adds on a cough. "Inter-dimensional Travels warps time. What feels like minutes passes in hours in the present world."

"You passed, but you failed, I'm afraid." Professor Zent licks his dry lips and drops his attention back to his papers. "Do try to do better next week on the semester final."

God dammit.

I wish I could say that's the worst thing that happens today.

White fuming smoke drifts from the front doors of Dorm J. It's late into the night and the twirling fiery scent of something burning drifts through the evening air, clouding over the nearly full moon above.

I stand at the front step, side by side with Phoenix. His fingers slide slowly into mine and it's the first real moment that I feel like we're a real team. Friends almost.

"Don't leave my side," he whispers, taking the first step on the broken concrete and guiding me into the ash that's drifting through the halls. It clings to our bodies, shadows against our skin, a sticky coating that comes off easily with the gentle brush of fingertips.

When I think of ash, I think of destruction, of consuming fire raging and destroying. Funny how something like the aftermath of flames can seem so gentle somehow. But where is it coming from?

Blood splatters the old brick walls. It lines the broken tile floor like a pathway of breadcrumbs left behind, as if something was dragged from the front doors all the way up to the fifth floor.

Our floor.

A shiver crawls down my spine, sweat clinging there with every step I take.

What happened here? In the eleven hours that we were gone, this place is in worse shape than before. And I didn't think that was possible.

My focus is room 503. My friends are in there. Saint and Malek are in there.

I hope.

Just when we creep cautiously up to it, the door directly across flings open. Violent steps storm toward me, black reckless eyes look to me with so much pain in them it's terrifying.

Syko's big arms wrap around me fully, pulling me against his hard chest until I can feel the tremble of his breaths inside. Slowly, Phoenix slides his hand away from mine and my fingers push through the downy soft feathers of the beautiful man wrapped around me.

"They fucking took her, Izara." A sinking feeling of rage and sadness thickens his rasping voice. "They fucking brought her to the most dangerous place for a startle Prod and then they fucking blamed her when her Prodigium lashed out." Hot breath heaves out from his trembling lips but he bites the uneven sound of his voice back. He's tensing in my arms and just clinging to me like I can fix all the terrible things the world has done to him.

To Kayos.

She didn't stand a chance.

EIGHTEEN

Izara

Thick hair meets my fingertips and I push his pale white locks back from the lost look in his big eyes. He's slept on my bed for four days now. He hasn't moved once.

And they've given no updates on Kayos.

The curl of his body fits against mine and I hold him against my chest, listening to the steady but slow rhythm of his breath.

This place tries to break us.

They broke Kayos. And now they're breaking Syko.

"You should get out for a few hours. Get some air," Saint says to me softly.

"No." Malek's bare shoulders hold steely posture, his dark hair hanging loosely around his handsome face.

I had no intention of leaving Syko.

But now I'm curious.

"Why?"

"Full moon," Malek says without further explanation.

I wait, but he gives me nothing more.

Okay...

My gaze spans to Phoenix sitting lazily across from me, his attention flicking from me to the nephilim holding me to him.

What are we? Are we really dating? Is this real for him?

The hard pull of his brows and the purse of his lips makes it feel real. The confusing guilt laying like lead in my stomach feels real.

"We should talk," I say to Phoenix flatly.

"Nothing to talk about." He shakes his head, biting the inside of his cheek, that *I don't give a fuck about anything or anyone* firmly in place against his features.

"You're an idiot," Saint whispers from the bunk above.

"If she wants to sleep fuck me, but in reality snuggle the bird boy, that's none of my business. We're *not real*." He air quotes that statement like it's our relationship slogan.

Phoenix and Izara, Keeping it Not Real Since 2019.

I hate this.

Maybe I do need to get out of this fucking room.

I don't leave right away. It's hard to extricate myself from

Syko's body. Any time I tried, he pulled me closer, as if his unconsciousness couldn't stand the thought of being alone without my warmth. It's as if somehow I understood above all others what his sister means to him, and it was only in me that he could find solace.

I hated to leave him, but I was suffocating as much as he was. He couldn't pull me close without Phoenix grunting or snorting or offering bitter commentary, to which Saint only replied in my defense. Malek had long since left the room. He never said where he was going and I didn't ask.

Which is exactly why I'm here.

My tennis shoes crunch against dry leaves and dead earth. The wind stings my face, making tears burn behind my eyelids and trail down my cheeks. I tell myself it has everything to do with the cold and nothing to do with the haunting loss in Syko's eyes echoing in my own heart.

"Your art is overemotional," Kayos had said to me.

She's right. *I'm* overly emotional and it comes out in a mess of reclusive quietness and lashing aggression sometimes. I'm wandering campus grounds with my hands shoved tightly into my pockets, crying silent tears over a young girl taken because she couldn't control the Prod inside her.

Maybe I'm crying for myself, because Kayos reminds me of me. Maybe I'm crying because we don't know if she's locked in confinement or if they killed her because of that power.

At this point, I don't know why the empty tears linger damply in my eyes.

I just know that I want to scream. The emotions are building inside me to painful proportions and I don't have a fucking outlet. If I were at home, I'd slather paint onto a canvas, onto a wall. I'd streak across it in violent brush strokes with wild music screaming in my ears. I'd jump from one canvas to the next, giving my emotions color and texture until I could make sense of it. Or maybe the point is to not make sense of it at all.

Maybe it's just that need for release.

And if I can't find paints, I have to do it some other way.

Storming into the woods I'd been in with Malek so long ago, I gather sticks and rocks, dig my fingers into the black earth to pull it out by clumps. I'm blind, with nothing but the soft moon lit rays of silver illumination to guide me from between thin branches. It's enough. I pile dirt as if it were clay, I bend sticks, stack rocks. I make art in its basest, rawest form.

I don't know how long I've been here. How long my numb fingers bleed as I give form to my emotions. Hours into the night. Hours in which the tears slide down my cheeks. In which the pain loosens bit by painful bit.

Until the slapping sting of the wind brings the first howl of a wolf to me and tears through the haze of my emotions.

My gaze tears across the vacant woods. To the sound of branches snapping, of feet rushing towards me.

I blink up at the full shining light of the moon.

"Full Moon."

Fuck.

NINETEEN

Malek

Every month it was the same, and every month it never got any easier; *the Change*. It was always a phantom kernel inside... at first. But as the days close in to the full moon, the Prod rips violently from the confines I keep it locked behind.

It claws and bites, tearing through the very foundations of my soul only to arise bloody and gnashing, as if to say "I am here now. And now, it's *my* turn."

One day a month I let it reign free.

There are shifters who train themselves to shift at will, with or without the help of the moon. I prefer not to. Not when the risks of doing so are deadly. Not when giving yourself to the beast inside merges both entities. Mind of the beast and man collide until it's impossible to tell one apart from the other.

It's why some werewolves are so feral. So violent.

I want to be better.

So it's on every full moon that I unleash my more violent self.

During the full moon, the Academy locks up the shifters with no control over themselves. They're sent away to the lowest level of Dormitory J, locked up like dogs in a kennel. The better students like me are allowed to roam the grounds. It's good for my Prod and it's good for me. Being here in nature, it eases the control, makes everything calmer.

It has taken every ounce of self control I have to prove to them I'm not the same out-of-control beast that ripped through my stepfather. Not like it had been my fault. He had known what I was. Had been given a fair warning. That didn't stop him from taunting my wolf until it tore an open wound in his neck, never mind the fact that he'd chained me up at the time.

I'm better than that.

I *have* to be better than that.

Maybe if I was, my mother, brothers, and pack wouldn't fear me anymore. I'd have a family again. I could have a normal relationship with Izzy. One where I didn't have to keep her at arm's length out of fear. One where I didn't have to hold back from pulling her close. From kissing her. From calling her mine.

It took me months to accept the feelings that my Prod had obsessed over from the very first second I laid eyes on Izara Castillo.

She's my mate.

And someday, I'll have enough control over my Prod to tell her that.

Thoughts of Izzy bring the beast hurtling forward.

Mine.

A growl rises painfully up my throat, more guttural than human.

I drop to my knees on the dirt. Twigs and rocks dig into my bare knees. When I fall to all fours, the rocks abrade my palms but that pain is *nothing* compared to the excruciating rippling of my skin as the Change takes over.

I dig my fingers into the cold earth. Nails crack and bleed, ripping from the quick while claws replace them. I feel my insides distorting, pushing at skin and bones with expanding force.

The air is frost kissed, and yet, my skin is burning up.

A violent tremor shudders through me. I arch, screaming into the night air only to have the sound transform into the howls of a beast.

Every muscle spasms. My skin bursts in red welts that melt from my body. Hair sprouts, bones and body elongate. The pain has me dry heaving into the dirt. There's nothing more painful than this.

Nothing but the memory of my kills.

Thank God I told Izzy to stay inside. As long as she stays with Phoenix and Saint, she's safe from me, safe from the beast that would claim her.

Mine.

His growl within my head is a demonic demand that rumbles through me.

In one shuddering explosion, my entire body changes in an instant. The skin rips from me in shreds until I'm a massive *thing*. A beast that stands on two back paws. A wolf that arches up and howls.

At long last.

It's me, and yet it's not. I know they say we are our Prods, that it is a part of us, so intricately woven into the fibers of our soul that we are one and the same. It is our DNA. It is us. I've said it to Izzy plenty of times. But every time I Change, the more logical part of me tries to reason with myself.

This is not me.

But it is.

These savage cravings, these wild instincts, they thrum inside me every fucking day. Every fucking day they beg for control. They beg for the tether to snap to make way for my more primitive instincts.

And tonight is the night they do.

Tonight is a night for running. For hunting. For *fucking*.

I drop to all fours and prowl the woods in hulking form. I start at a slow walk and then my paws move of their own volition. Soon, I am running and branches crack under my feet. This is freedom in its rawest form. It's everything I crave, everything I long for.

The cold wind whistles through my fur just faintly. My ears pick up every delicate sound. From the hoot of night owls, to the soft padding of other shifters. I steer clear of them. I know they are as vicious as I am tonight and won't hesitate to rip through me if I invade their territory. Though my body is itching for a fight, I'm still smart enough to avoid it. I listen to every sound like a song I've long forgotten.

The wind shifts direction, bringing me the scent of familiarity. Of ink and sweat. Of fear and sorrow. Of long dark hair and golden-brown eyes that hold friendship and love in equal measure.

Mine.

I scent her before I see her, before I hear her.

And it fills the primitive part of me with rage and satisfaction. She's here, she came.

Mine. Mine. Mine.

I told her to stay away. Why didn't she listen? Does she *want* to get killed?

Mine.

I told her what would happen. I told her it was the full moon. She knew, and she came anyway.

Mine.

And now the beast is ready to claim her.

And the tether on my control snaps completely.

If she wanted a beast, then the beast is what she'll get.

I fucking warned her, after all...

TWENTY

Izara

There's nothing in the way of protection except for an unsturdy branch and the dormant, useless Prod deep inside me.

Fuck.

I could bring it forth if I had to. I'd force the reckless thing to come out if it meant life and death.

The smarter option here would be to run. But even I'm smart enough to know I can't outrun the approaching werewolf. Besides, they smell fear. They love the chase. And I'm not giving the beast the satisfaction.

The steps of the wolf come closer. Sweat and fear cling to me like a second skin. My hands tighten so hard on the branch my palms scrape painfully.

Twigs snap. Closer. The beast is coming closer. My breaths grow labored in my chest, and my heart pounds so hard I can hear the echoes of it around the quiet night.

I bring the branch up like a baseball bat, search inside myself for that power, for the violence of the Prod that has the ability to tear people apart.

Fear ripples through me as the thin tree branches part and an enormous brown wolf prowls through.

It's so different from what I thought it would be. The spine arches the way a human's would as it stalks on all fours with an animalistic sway to its step, but it looks like it's every bit as capable of standing impossibly tall on its strong back legs.

I freeze stupidly in my fear as the yellow eyes of the beast settle over me. My breaths are shallow, painful gasps.

The beast snarls, and the sound breaks me out of my daze. I can't win against this. There's no fucking way.

My footsteps slide against the cold grass for a single second. It just a split moment of stumbling unsteadiness. And then I sprint like my life literally depends on it.

My legs pump beneath me, thighs screaming with every painful step. I don't pay attention to the pain. I dodge the copse of trees, even as branches slap my face and slice my skin. I push forward with the snarls and snapping of the beast behind me. All I can focus on is the little hints of lights beyond the woods.

Never has the Academy looked so safe.

But I'll never make it.

A moment later, enormous paws slam into my back and I sprawl to the ground. My teeth clatter from the shock, and the weight of the wolf digging into me presses my chest into the dirt. It's painful, and panic sets in as the wolf looms over me.

Snarling warm breath burns across my cheek as I take shallow, careful breaths.

I try not to move, try not to panic. But fuck, wet tears are filling my eyes because I know I'll die here tonight.

The body above mine shifts, and then a cracking sound splinters through my ears. The growls and whines become the groans of man and the heavy weight lessens, but is still there hovering.

I can't make eye contact with it, I can't move, I can't even think.

Warm hands slide up my arms to capture my wrists and hold me to the ground. This is worse. This is by far worse than having a wolf above me. I want to scream but terror paralyzes the sound in my throat.

Hot breath fans along my ear.

Then the deep curl of accented words send relief shuddering through me. "I thought I told you to stay inside tonight, Izara."

"*Malek.*" I breathe his name like a prayer.

"Why are you here, Izzy?" he growls.

There's uncontrolled anger in his tone but his hands and body are pressing into me in a very, very different way.

His lips are on my skin. In fact, his whole body is becoming intimate with mine, and my skin is memorizing the feel of his bare flesh against the back of my thighs, against the curve of my ass. I feel his every muscle wound tightly, straining for control.

"I told you it was too dangerous to come."

The way he says 'come' makes my body hum with awareness. It's only now that I realize how hard he is. It's only now I realize the strain of his cock is pressing against my skirt and his hips are grinding me harder into the dirt.

My body shivers with sudden a wave of want.

This is dangerous.

This is sexy.

This isn't the Malek I know. The Malek I know is safe and kind. He's gentle and caring. He keeps me at arm's length and offers me quiet, tentative smiles.

Malek presses his lips firmly to my neck, slipping his tongue right over my pulse. His mouth opens fully and the sharp canines of his teeth graze over my flesh.

My whole body trembles as he sets off pleasurable sensation after sensation inside me.

"You shouldn't have fucking come, Izzy."

His words are a warning I heed all too late, or not at all. There's no regret in them, just endless expanse of painful desire. A desire I feel down to my core.

I shift, my thighs rubbing together bring me the slightest bit of relief. But the hard ridge of his cock against my backside only makes me crave more.

"But now that you're here..." His voice just gets darker, more dangerous with each slow drawl of his low, rumbling words. His teeth rake across my jawline and he melds closer, leaning over me so his mouth touches the corner of my lips. "... I'm not going to let you go."

Those taunting words make demanding need click into place all through my body.

I turn my head and meet his kiss, passion for passion. He's feral in his exploration, as his tongue dives into my mouth to claim me for his own.

This isn't the Malek I know. I remind myself again.

Fuck, but I'd like to know more of him. I want to know his every aspect in the joining of our bodies, in slick flesh against flesh.

And Full Moon Malek seems ready to give me every single thing I ask for.

He tears away long enough to growl, "You're mine, Izara Castillo. *Mine.*"

I don't bother to question or contradict him because in this moment, I *feel* like I'm his. Wholly and entirely, in this moment I belong to this primitive side of him. My first friend and now something more. Our friendship has changed eternally now. Now he can't keep me at bay ever again.

"*Yesss...*" It comes out as a hiss when his teeth bite the soft lobe of my ear, trembling a tingling sensation right down to my core. Every touch, every swipe of his tongue makes me burn with need.

"Say it, Izzy." His hips grind against the thin material of my panties, while his lips caress me and his hands hold my wrists down.

His big body is dominating me completely.

And I love every fucking second of it.

"I'm yours," I groan, jerking my ass back to meet his cock. I want my clothes to fall away. I want the burn of his touch.

"Say my *name*." His hand releases me to slide down my body. He squeezes one mound of my ass briefly before he's jerking my skirt down and over my legs, pushing it past my shoes. *"Say it."* He fingers the edge of my panties, rocking back and forth, teasing the smooth skin half an inch from my opening.

Fuck, I wish I had something prettier than the cotton panties provided by the Academy, the golden shield emblem and all slapped across my ass.

He doesn't seem to care either way. He plays with the edges, fingers slipping inside to caress the warmth of my folds for mere seconds before sliding away all over again.

"I'm *yours*, Malek. I'm yours. *Fuck. Please.*"

The tattering rip of fabric cuts through the night as he tears the panties straight off of my body.

And I don't even care because I need him.

But Malek is thorough in his ministrations. His movements are firm, each touch of his fingertips is like a fresh brand across my skin. His rough palms slide down to cup my ass. He groans as he plays, his fingers molding my figure into his palms.

"*Mine.* My mat—." He cuts the words off strangely with a deadly snarl.

His gentle touch suddenly collides hotly against my ass, and the stinging feeling spirals through my body on waves. I gasp, jerking forward, nails curling into the cold dirt.

When his fingers slide down the back of me, parting and searching until he presses hard over my clit, I cry out.

"I wanted to spare you from the beast," he growls, and I can't help but notice the raw guttural sound of it. It only makes all of this more erotic. "But there's no going back now."

His fingers dive inside me, stretching the walls of my sex. He moves, in and out. The slickness of his fingers is sensual and arches just right. He has me panting within moments, quivering against the ground while he fucks me slowly with his hand.

"Fuck," he groans, and then his nails dig into my hips and lift them up so I'm on my knees, displayed before him on all fours.

This is primitive. Primal.

And I want every bit of it.

He bends low until his head dips behind me and the first rasp of his tongue sliding up my folds almost sends me spiraling. The air catches in my lungs and then I'm rocking against his mouth as he tastes me, his tongue diving into me and exploring.

My every gasp is a plea to go faster, harder. His fingers dance around to tease, pressing diligent circles into my clit over and over and over again, until I feel myself rising high...

And then the feeling fades.

Malek pulls away, kneeling behind me, aligning his hips with my ass.

"Look at me, Izara."

I bite my lip but obey, afraid I'll beg if I don't. My body is already shaking with need, but the sight of his eyes glowing feral and yellow in the moonlight makes me whimper.

This is a new Malek.

A Malek who controls every bit of my body with delicious commanding sensations.

"This won't be gentle," he warns, and even if his words warn of the contrary, there's a soft conflicting hum in the words, caring beneath the primal pleasure. "I am going to fuck you until the only thing you remember is my name. Until you beg for my mercy." He palms the underside of his dick and slides it over me, poising it at my entrance. He leans forward, his bare chest brushing my back. "And even as you beg for mercy, I won't grant it."

Good.

Because I want every bit of the beast right now.

And then he slides into me in one hard thrust.

He fills me so entirely, so thoroughly, that my orgasm spirals through me fast and hard. I shudder beneath him even as he thrusts harder from behind, holding my hips steady as he pounds faster and faster. He's relentless, almost violent in a way that's too filled with pleasure to have a single hint of pain. It's like for so long he's held himself back from doing just this.

And now that he has me, he seems to be intent on letting the frost-bitten wind carry my shaking cries into the endless expanse of the darkness around us.

His hands reach around me and slip beneath my jacket and shirt to tease my nipples. He brushes over them fully with his palms before he pinches them abruptly and the tingling energy builds inside me all over again. His hand drifts down lower, slipping over my skin until he makes his way to the front of my sex. He pushes over my slickness where his dick thrusts hard inside me, at the edge of where our bodies meets. His thumb trails circles around my clit and it's too much, too soon, and I'm coming again.

I drop to my elbows in the dirt. The waves of release are too much and I can't keep myself upright even if I want to. His hands support my hips, never releasing me, as he finds his bliss inside me. And even when he does, he doesn't stop. He continues that tormenting building sensation, filling me entirely until everything else falls away completely. There's nothing except for his cock inside me, the slick feel of him sliding in and out, roughly rocking against my inner walls.

His energy seems endless, and I absorb every bit of it, every moment of his rasping breath, of the roughness of his chest against my back, of bare skin on bare skin. My hips slam back to meet his in a dance neither of us know the steps to, but are too caught up in each other to care.

I thought the intensity of it all was impossible up until this point, but it builds all over again, higher, until

I'm panting beneath him, arching and curling into his body on uncontrollable trembling movements.

"*Malek*," his name escapes my lips on a hissing, moaning breath. Just as I'm about to spiral toward that unreachable crash, he pulls back to deny it from me.

"Please, Malek." My fingers drag into the dirt, nails cracking at the pain and torturous perfection of it all.

He hums a content sounding groan at the plea but never stops.

He moves faster, as if it could never be enough. One hand slips from my hip and slides up my spine to tangle into the roots of my long hair. He tugs, and the sting of the gesture only fuels every tumultuous emotion that rages inside of me. He pulls until I'm sitting up, until I'm practically in his lap and he dives into me from behind and beneath me.

Relentless. Passionate. Everything he kept so tightly locked up he unleashes onto me in vicious wave after wave of consuming sensations.

The heat of our bodies mingle as his hard chest slides along my spine, his strong arms wrapping around me in complete strength.

I turn to his kiss, biting at his bottom lip so he can feel the frustration building inside me with every thrust of my tongue against his. Together we taste like earth and sweat and tears, and nothing has ever been more delicious or wildly out of control.

I suck his bottom lip into my mouth. There's no perfection in our movements, no slow seduction. This chaotic harmony is better than that, and it's everything I never knew I needed. His hand slips down my ribs on a slow path that he's memorized now, sliding right to my clit to build that reckless energy he keeps drawing out of me.

"Come, Izzy" he growls against my lips. "*Now*."

The growling demand alone tingles through my core.

His body commands my own, and I fall into that chasm of pleasure, screaming his name into the darkness only to finally hear him follow in the end with rough, hard and deep strokes that have him almost collapsing against me. His growls turn into howls as he slowly slips his cock from the slick tightness of my body, making me feel like I lost some essential part of myself because of his absence. Hot, heavy breaths wash over my neck as he pulls me closer, as if we could merge together somehow, his beautiful, deadly Prod and mine.

"Fuck, Izzy." Every word is becoming more beastly. "You... need... to leave. *Now*." The warmth of his body slips from mine momentarily before he's lifting me up by the hips.

I can barely stand and there's an ache between my thighs that makes my legs tremble. I would have been content to lie in our perfect bliss and dream about all the things he just made me feel, but Malek has different ideas, and cuddling is not one of them.

His every movement is jerky as he grasps my skirt and pulls it up my shaking legs, settling it on my hips. He's kneeling in front of me, his every muscle rippling like he's some bronze god rising from the earth to worship me.

He looks up at me. His dark locks are plastered to his temples and forehead. Without his glasses, he looks younger. The hint of his beastly change clings to him like smoke. The carefully constructed control that was missing as he fucked me is back, and it looks like it's taking every bit of will he has to keep the beast in check.

"I don't want to hurt you." His lips skim across my stomach, his words muffled behind the material of my shirt. I feel his heat through the material of my clothes. His entire body is burning up. "You need to leave."

My hands scrape through his soft tufts of hair. I've never taken these liberties with Malek before. I've never simply felt his soft dark locks.

Things are different now.

And I'm going to touch him now the way I've always wanted to.

"You won't hurt me." I bend down and press a kiss to his forehead. "You wanted me to be yours right?" I ask hesitantly, barely certain of what we said or what he promised. "I don't believe you'd ever hurt what's yours, Malek."

The breath that leaves him ripples through the entire length of his body. He drops his forehead to my stomach and takes in a few calming breaths, sending shivers through my body just from how intimately he's holding me.

"You're right." His fingers slip between the spaces of

mine. When he pulls away, there are depths of pain in the darkness of his eyes that physically hurts. "But I'm not ready for you to see me like this. And... there are still wolves here that could harm you. I won't let them touch you, *mi corazón*."

The endearment brings a tangle of heavy emotions through my chest for a reason I don't understand.

My heart.

When he said I was his, he meant it in all its entirety. His woman. His *heart.*

It is endearing and overwhelming all at the same time.

"I'll go back." I cup his cheek.

He nods. "Walk straight. I'll protect you from the shadows. Go into the dorm and don't come back out. Promise me."

"I promise."

His body ripples again and he gives me a light shove. "Go," he orders, dropping to all fours, his big hands fisting into the dirt.

I catch a glimpse of welts rising along his flesh and a hint of brown fur. His skin starts shredding as if invisible claws are raking through his body.

He lets out a howl of pain.

"Go!"

I turn away, no matter how hard it is, no matter how badly my body trembles and protests, I push myself faster through the woods. I shove aside branches and break away from the trees. The sad sight of the crumbling school buildings awaits me, yet I pause and half turn.

Howls pierce the night sky. A warning of a promise I must keep.

So I turn and run for Dorm J, the echoing cries of Malek's howls following me the entire way.

TWENTY-ONE

Izara

"You smell like wet dog."

As far as terrible greetings go, this one is pretty high up there. Fucking incubus and the fucking jealousy and possession that gleams in his obnoxiously beautiful eyes.

It's barely daylight outside, and he's just sitting here facing the door like he's waiting for me.

He's sitting up on his bunk, his feet kicking back and forth like a child who doesn't give a damn what monsters might lurk beneath his bed.

Aside from his constantly pouty attitude, he's anything but a child. Massive, bulky arms cross against the perfection that is his chest, wisps of red hair fall against his temple and black demonic eyes that should be frightening, but are more annoying than anything, look up at me.

Saint sits up in bed as I close the door behind me

with a cry of the hinges. The vampire's appearance holds traces of sleep, his dark hair standing up on end, boxers askew against his lean hips. Everything about him is lazy except his bright eyes, which are alight with glee and devilry.

The only one with his eyes closed is Syko, who lies on my bunk with his palms splayed gentle over his abdomen. I know he's awake, and aware of me by the tension that's lining his tired face. I'm just not sure he can bring himself to care. Or maybe he does care. I don't know. I'm confused, my body still rushing with the adrenaline that Malek's touch provoked.

He meant it. He told me to say I was his, and that claim was more than just words to him.

I don't know how I feel about that.

My thighs quiver. Shit, I want to fall to the ground and sleep but I have to change. I'm not wearing any panties, and my thighs are damp with pleasure and pain.

I ignore Phoenix's charming comment and go over to the closet, pulling out a fresh pair of Academy of Six cotton panties and a clean gym t-shirt that doubles as pajamas. I really just want my own clothes.

My own things.

Anything.

"I can smell him on you, you know? I can smell sex all over you."

Jesus fuck, there is absolutely no privacy, no sense of personal space in this fucking dorm. In this fucking school. All my secrets are bared out for everyone now, and why the fuck does Phoenix care, anyway?

"Did the mutt knot you real good?"

Anger slices through me as I whirl around. "Knotting is not a thing for werewolves."

I can't help but pause... *is it?*

"And besides, what do you care who I fuck, Phoenix?"

His long legs stand and he's prowling the short distance over to me. His danger, anger, and violence hums around the room like the striking of a cord. I almost wish he'd push me. I'm so emotional I'll push back. Everyone else might be afraid of the big bad incubus, but I'm not.

He looms over me, so close I can see the glare in his gaze, the tightness in his jaw. "You are *my* girlfriend," he growls. "Will you let everyone fuck you while I watch?" His palms grip the front of my thighs and he spreads them. His forceful touch burns across my skin, and as he said, the traces of sex still cling to me, and this violence is infinitely more erotic than it should be.

Maybe that's the most savage thing inside me, the darkest part of my soul. I crave violence like candy. Maybe that's why my Prod can tear people apart.

Because deep down, beneath the quiet exterior, I fucking enjoy it.

It's the only explanation I have for relishing in Phoenix's touch even after Malek already buried himself deep inside me, after he already claimed me.

The incubus's palms push fully over the sensitive skin of my inner thighs and I just want to push him as much as he always pushes me.

"Is that your kink? Watching?" I hold the clothes between us like some feeble barrier and tighten my fingers around them so he can't see I'm trembling. "Is that what really pisses you off, Phoenix? That you didn't get to watch someone else fuck me until I came again and again and again against his cock?"

His palms slide further up my thighs, pushing up my skirt and coming dangerously close to my center. Just a single slip of his fingers higher and he'll be touching my wetness. I want it, almost as much as I wanted Malek. I want it as much as I want this infuriating demon to kiss me.

But I want him to suffer even more.

My chin tips higher, his gaze dropping to my lips that are so, so close to his.

"Watching will be your only chance to ever see me like that." I swallow hard and he watches every emotion I'm hiding deep down inside, but I give him one more quiet promise. "Because I'm never touching you again." I turn and push open the door of the bathroom, slamming it in his face. As soon as he's out of sight, I lean against the door, slumping into it.

I'm so fucking exhausted. From everything. From life.

I am going to fuck you until the only thing you remember is my name.

A shiver drives through me at the memory of his dark rasping voice.

I stand on shaking legs and look at myself in the mirror, unsurprised at what I find there. I look like I've been thoroughly fucked. My hair is a tangle of dark locks, threaded through with twigs, my dirt stained cheeks are sticky with tears and my neck is covered in the soft indentations of his teeth marks.

He branded me as much as he claimed me it seems.

I shouldn't like it.

I shouldn't.

But I do.

I strip quickly, my thighs sticky with the remnants of Malek and the pleasure we both experienced. It's intimate in every way and I wonder if things changed for him as much as they did for me. If he'll continue to push me away or if what happened between us will now bring us closer.

In every possible way.

TWENTY-TWO

Phoenix

Parent's day. One of the lucky days a year that our parents get to visit.

Unless your parents are unknown. When you fuck a lot, you have a lot of kids you don't have time to care about. You know, because you have so much fucking to do you just can't be bothered with raising a kid.

I get it. My parents, whoever they were, had other shit to do.

It happens to a lot to demons. I'm stronger because of it.

My arms fold as I watch my fake girlfriend jump through hoops for the man who apparently raised her when her real parents checked out.

Her dark eyes lift to me and the smile on her lips almost slips away.

We're safely back to pretending. I'm back to

pretending I've completely gotten the image of Malek fucking her out of the darkest parts of my mind.

I tried to avoid her. I tried so fucking hard.

But it hurts. It physically fucking hurts in my chest where pure numbness used to reside.

Because of this Prodless woman.

And I still get these terrible fucking feelings in my stomach when she's around. Like I want to dry heave and giggle endlessly all at the same time.

Butterflies. Saint says they're butterflies.

The feck gave me a contagious case of the butterflies and now it's like I'm addicted to her hate. Which is why I'm still pretending.

And so is she.

She leads her father from the chaos of the halls and into the quietness of our dorm room where I stand alone.

Lucky me.

"Dad, this is my... *boyfriend.*" She nearly gags just saying that last word, and I'd be a fucking liar if I didn't admit how hard that gag sound just made my cock.

I lift my hand swiftly and even if I am an asshole, I do know how to be a respectful asshole. Especially to people who deserve it. And this guy, this guy took in an unknown Prod when no one else wanted her, he more than deserves my respect.

He doesn't take my hand immediately. He also takes his time eyeing me slowly. The man's blonde mustache shifts as he inhales deeply through his nose. "Demon born?" he asks with suspicion coating his words.

He finally takes my hand, giving it a hard squeeze that I think is meant to pain me.

I shake briefly, both of us eyeing one another in a strange way now.

"I'm a soulless, actually." I leave out the incubus part because I'm sure the last thing dear old dad wants to know is that I want to fuck his daughter non stop until she's a brainless puddle of sex on my mattress.

"Soulless, what does that mean exactly? How dangerous are you?" He's nearly standing between me and Izzy now and I see where this is going.

"It means I was born without a soul. It happens occasionally to demons. It mostly just causes a divide between our actions and emotions. I'm not good at feeling a lot of normal things most people do."

I've become good at reciting through that little list. I've said it in my head often enough. I should just walk around with an introduction sticker that tells everyone I'm a face value asshole and get it over with.

Because that's what he wants to hear.

I fold my arms and I'm surprised when his little princess slides her small palm across the lowest part of my back. A tingle of unexplainable warmth sears over me everywhere her small body touches mine. That dry heave giggle threatens to crawl up my chest and throat again.

I both hate and love that she can do that to me.

Every. Single. Time.

Why?

Why the hell have I fucked a thousand women, and

this one feck has the ability to turn me into a whipped demon waiting at her beck and call?

She leans into me, her perfect breasts pressing into my side before she presses a quick kiss to my tense jaw line.

My head tilts slowly to her, still not holding her, still confused as hell why she's pretending so well for her father.

"He's really sweet, Daddy." Her small palm glides across my rigid arm and still I just stare at the confusing girl at my side.

She fucked my roommate yesterday.

She fucked Malek.

And now she's here making my soul want to pound and my lungs want to ache for air.

What the fuck is wrong with me?

It's like she and I live to torment each other.

And right now, she's better at it than I am.

"Is he keeping you safe, Izara? These people, they're dangerous. They're not like the humans we grew up around. My magic can't protect you here. I don't practice anymore but I would. You know I would, to keep you safe." His wide gaze swivels around to the open doorway of our dorm at all the creatures passing by.

The Prod down the hall, with antlers spouting right from his skull, strides past our room and her father visibly shivers.

He just wants to know Izzy is okay.

My palm pushes down the small of her back and she

stiffens just slightly as I pull her fully up against me, my gaze searching the deep whiskey amber of her eyes.

"I won't let anything happen to her, Mr. Castillo."

"*Thomson*. Castillo is Izara's family name," he tells me. But when he looks back at me, all that judgement is gone. "Family is important. Her heritage—" he pauses abruptly before correcting himself, "—her Mexican heritage is important. Izara is important."

Her family history is important but her supernatural history isn't?

Mr. Thomson is a strange, strange man as far as Warlocks go.

"I'm glad she has you," he finally says with a small smile forcing to his lips.

Izzy settles into my chest at the simple sound of her father's approval and I don't know why I'm fucking preening over his words too.

This boyfriend shit is not for me.

"I have to go. They told me five minutes and I'm running into minute seven as we speak, dear." His slender frame towers over us and he gives her a loose side hug that she melts into.

"Bye, Daddy."

"I'll see you soon. You'll be done with your two years in no time," he whispers rather sadly. "But in the meantime..." He pulls away and shrugs a backpack from his shoulders, handing it to her by the strap. "I was able to bring you a few things I thought you might need."

A squeal pierces past her lips as she aggressively

yanks the zippers open one handed and rummages through the contents inside. She whips out shirts and jeans, panties, socks, and paint splattered brush after brush in all varying sizes.

"I didn't have time to grab your paints. Sorry."

The bag and contents fall to the floor with a quiet thought. "This is more than enough. Thanks Daddy."

They fall into another loose embrace.

And still she holds on to me. Holding me to her as she clings to him.

She's small. Weak.

A complete feck.

And she truly needs me.

When he slips out of our room with a screech of the hinges, we're alone.

I shake my head at the weirdness that is her father and my lips part to tell her just that.

But then she's arching against me, and her mouth is against mine, soft and hesitant.

And I crack under the light pressure of that sweet mouth of hers.

"I'm sorry," she murmurs, but my tongue flicks her apology away like I never want to taste that word against her lips ever again.

The way my fingers dig into her hips makes her whimper but she only clings to me even harder. Every brush of our lips, every roll of her tongue, every drag of her nails against my skin isn't enough.

I slam her back against the wall so hard the door rattles at our side.

The heavy moan that hums against my lips from her needy mouth is too much for me to handle. It's too much for something that isn't real.

She makes me feel *too much*.

I pull back from her with a shaking breath pushing from my lungs.

"I'm sorry," she whispers again.

I kiss those words away once more.

"I'm sorry," I tell her firmly. "I'm sorry I acted like any of this is real."

The delicate arch of her brows pulls together.

"Is it?" Her fingers push through my hair and those big eyes of hers devour all the things I haven't even said yet.

"It's not." I say one thing but I can't help but do another. My lips press over hers. "I don't own you. Me and you, and the things we do together aren't real, Izzy."

The shit I feel inside for you, that consuming, terrifying feeling, that's not real.

"Then why are we still kissing?" She nips at my bottom lip hard and I groan against her mouth.

"It's called pretending, Iz." My hips rock into hers and she lifts her leg against my hip until all I feel is her addicting warmth pressed right against my cock.

"Who are we pretending for?" she asks on a shaking breath.

I kiss her distracting question away once more with a slow flick of my tongue.

"*Us.* We're pretending for me and for you and for anyone else who might want to watch."

As much as she terrifies me, she captivates me too.

And I'd rather pretend for just a little while with this ridiculous, sexy, annoying, perfect woman, than feel nothing at all.

TWENTY-THREE

Syko

The incubus is in my spot. Not that it's my spot, really. It's Izzy's bed. She's allowed to cuddle up with filthy demons who will leave her sheets smelling like burnt bacon if that's what she wants.

The demon's bright eyes shift to me leaning against the wall, blatantly watching them but not having the control to look away.

He arches an eyebrow at me before dipping his head low and pressing slow, teasing kisses to her mouth. It's almost enough to make me flop down on the other side of her just to see if he'd still have the balls to keep pushing me.

And to see how she'd respond, if I'm being honest.

The way she slides her leg over his hips and just slightly rocks her center against him makes me wonder if she'd even notice if there was a third fucking person on that tiny cot.

"Didn't you hate him three days ago?" I grind out, my arms folding hard across my chest. I'm pretty sure that was them arguing loud and clear and now they're dry humping in front of me.

Lovely.

She nods but her mouth never leaves his, his fucking hands push down low until he's fully cupping her ass against him.

Why the fuck am I here?

"I—I" she smiles as he sucks her lower lip into his mouth and makes her hip buck harder against him. "I'm still mad at him."

Now both of them are smiling at each other.

And I'm dying. As we speak I'm gouging my eyes out in the corner with one of the wooden crosses Saint has decorated the room with.

His mother was a devout nun. Or so he says.

I can't even glance around the room because my gaze hasn't left Izara in almost thirty minutes.

"Take a nap with me," Phoenix whispers, his mouth trailing down her neck, her dark lashes fluttering as her fingers dig into his big neck.

A nap? Is that code for something? Is that a position? *The Nap...* what the fuck does that mean?

"I'm not fucking you, Phoenix. You and me, we're not real."

Yeah. I'm physically nodding along, an encouraging viewer that she doesn't even notice.

"That's not what I asked," he hums, running his nose slowly along the curve of her neck.

Shit. Even I can see that she's not strong enough to withstand an incubus.

Probably has a magic cock or something. Made of hellfire and sinner's lust.

Why. The fuck. Am I still here?

"Just take a nap with me," he pleads, his fucking hell-fire cock straining beneath his boxers as he subtly presses it against her stomach.

Jesus, he's an inch easy from giving her bellybutton an orgasm.

Fuck off already.

"Syko, will *you* take a nap with me? You looked tired." She twists away from him and the incubus's mouth drops open with clear annoyance on the tip of his tongue but the smile I give her is pure happy vengeance.

Fucking soulless.

"I am so tired, Izzy." I lay it on strong with the biggest black puppy dog eyes she's probably ever seen.

Her brows pull together with blatant concern and when she holds her hand out to me I don't waste a single second before dropping down on her other side and splaying my arms wide behind my head, making sure my elbows dig right into the side of demon fuck's meaty neck.

"Aww this is nice," she coos her body pressing along mine but her hands never really consoling me.

That's okay. Phoenix's death glare is consoling enough. Just knowing that I'm pissing all over the sex cacoon he was building is reward enough for me.

My palm slips beneath his big arms, wrapping around her hips and... Yep now my head's on his shoulder, death glare in full effect.

The sex cacoon is nice. We should have done this years ago.

"You know, you're not really my type," Phoenix grinds out, his arms tensing above mine but never moving.

He refuses to move. I refuse to move. We're both almost happy and almost miserable all at the same time.

"You're not mine either," I whisper and then to really fuck with him my hand slides to the lowest part of her back before adding, "I much prefer petite Prodless women with nice asses."

He's glaring so hard that vein at the side of his head is going to burst.

"If you two don't stop, I'll leave you to let you snuggle your frustrations out alone."

I smirk at her and my heart flares with an unbearable warmth when she pushes her palm across my abs and pulls me impossibly closer into our sex cacoon.

My eyes close slowly and it really is the calmest I've felt in days. The calmest I've felt since everything happened.

It's peaceful. So peaceful, I drift to sleep.

The strangest dream fills my restless thoughts. Phoenix strides from the shadows, walking from the darkness like he created it.

Weirdest of all, he's completely fucking naked.

"You wanted in on the nap, right?" A reckless smile pulls his lips back from his straight white teeth.

And then *I'm* naked.

And the fucking incubus is looking at me with so much sadistic happiness it's terrifying. In a flash he's right in my face, black eyes big enough to consume all the color from the world within their pools, teeth sharp enough to devour every emotion in my soul.

His palm drops between us and a scream tears up my throat when his fingers wrap around my dick. I shove back from him but I can't move from the tightness of the eerie darkness pressing in around us.

Pain strikes through every inch of my body starting with the slicing feeling his touch is stabbing into my shaft.

"Fuck with my nap time again and I'll make an exception about you not being my type, Christian Cock Block."

His hand jars back and I swear he takes something near and dear to my heart with him but just as he rears back, manic smile on place, I wake.

And fall right off the bed and onto the floor.

Harsh breaths push from my lungs as I look up at the nicotine stained ceiling. All I can do is lie there for several seconds, reliving the eerily realistic dream play-by-play.

Something moves above me, and messy hair, bright eyes, and a taunting smile look down on me.

"How was your nap?" Phoenix whispers.

My jaw clenches.

Fucking incubus tried to rip my dream dick off.

What the fuck.

If only that was enough to stop me from crawling right back in bed with her, passing him a wink before I wrap both arms around her and pull her small body right up against me.

She gives a breathy sigh that fans across my neck, her chin nuzzling into the crook of my neck. It calms my drilling heartbeat. Even if Phoenix is still imagining my dickless nudity in his glaring green eyes.

She has no fucking idea what we all put up with just to be near her.

And she probably never will.

Because she'll never see me the way she sees all of them. I'm the safe one. The good one. *The friend.*

That's exactly why she cares about me.

And that's all that matters.

For now.

TWENTY-FOUR

Izara

Everything is settling now. Malek still holds a distance between us. He hasn't mentioned claiming me or what happened that night. It's like there's something he can't tell me.

And it's straining between us.

Small touches pass here and there but he won't so much as kiss me.

Something's holding him back.

I just hope it's not me. I hope he's not afraid of all the answers I can't give him. It'd be so much easier for him to settle down with another werewolf. Any other Prod really.

Yet, he's with me day in and day out, smiling and helping and touching me but never really being with me.

Not the way I want.

And Phoenix...I just don't even know. I don't know what is going on in my love life.

That's not even what it is. Something this messy can't be called a love life.

The only good news is that finals aren't as bad as the teachers made them out to be. I can say with honesty and a small bit of pride that I'm not the worst student at the academy. We've lost so many failing Prods like Kayos, that the stress of being taken for any little thing drills into me with every exam I take.

But so far so good.

I can do this.

Miraculously, I pass every class so far. My grades aren't as good as Malek's or even Phoenix's—who knew my fake boyfriend was such a nerd?—but at least I won't be getting the boot.

Yet.

Interdimensional Travels makes me want to throw up in an assortment of different realms and dimensions but luckily I hold it together.

Malek catches my hand when I walk past, just a reassuring brush of our fingers and it calms the rising anxiety within me.

Or at least it does until I'm side by side with a man who barely glances my way when I pull out the chair next to him.

Phoenix and I are... okay. Just not good.

His emotions are just as confusing as mine lately.

I wish we could just spell all of this out for everyone.

Maybe I should distance myself from all of them. Would I be able to withstand the loss of all of them over the agony of having to choose just one of them?

I swallow that thought down as I lower myself into the seat next to his and he shifts slightly so our elbows don't have the accidental misfortune of brushing.

Definitely not doing great in lover's paradise

Professor Zent eyes us all one by one.

And then he lifts his long black wand and hovers it directly over his golden time piece. Particles gleam out of it and swirl in the air. The magic dances and sways before he lifts it higher and showers his watching class with...

"Is that pixie dust?" I ask with a curl of my lips.

"It's Wizard's Watch, Miss Izara. Today's final will be timed. You and your partner have exactly five minutes to enter your dimension, collect a small object and return."

"You—you want me to steal something from hell?"

"If that is where your heart takes you, Miss Izara, then by all means, bring me back a nice hot cup of demon's Coffee. Just be sure to return before your sparking dust turns to fiery embers and burns. *If you fail*," his monotone words ring out like an announcement at a Met's game, "you will not return until the embers turn to ash and my magic dissolves away entirely."

"How long does that take?" Saint asks at the table across from me, his eyes narrowed accusingly on the Professor.

"In your Interdimensional Travels, it could take no more than three hours. In this realm's time, it takes about two years."

Two years.

My wide eyes are pinned on the old man and his careless stature.

"The best of luck to you all. Your time starts," a short glance at his pocket watch, "*now.*"

I barely glance at Phoenix before he grips my hand and we flash away in less than a second like he's too impatient to even consult me.

My shoes stumble over the dirt and big hands catch me at the waist, pulling me against him before my nose skims the flickering hot flames.

"Center ring again. You're starting to look like a show off now, Izzy." His voice hums through me and I force myself to step away from his strength and stand on my own two feet.

"Okay. I need something to take back." My gaze shifts over the soot at our feet.

It's not dirt at all.

It's ash.

I blink vacantly at the thought of what could have made this much ash. What nasty things did they burn down here to line this entire hellacious hall with a garden of ash?

"You might have to keep walking to get an actual object." Phoenix doesn't glance at me but his stance is so close to mine that he brushes my body with his with every small breath he takes.

Before he didn't want our elbows to get too romantically involved and now that we're in hell, his obnoxiously hard chest is glued to my shoulder.

I think he might be hormonal. Do soulless demons go through puberty differently than the rest of the population?

I shake his confusing behavior off.

We take slow soundless steps down the hall, flames flickering across his features and making him look every bit like a creation of sin.

What does that say about me?

"Why do you think I keep coming back here?" I ask.

"To hell?"

"Yes, to hell. Where else would here mean?"

"I thought you might be questioning why you keep coming back to me."

It's always about Phoenix. Even when it's not. Even when it's about me, it's still about the selfish soulless incubus.

I roll my eyes and try again.

"Do you think I'm a demon?"

"You're definitely heartless enough, baby."

My head turns slowly so I can really fully appreciate my glare against his ridiculously handsome face.

The asshole.

"Do you think you could plot this out with me for a single second?"

He sighs dramatically. "You're a higher demon. Specifically, one who's powerful enough to bring us to a forbidden circle in hell. Is that what you wanted to hear?"

The soft sinking of my white shoes sliding against the ash halts. My heartbeat pounds so hard in my chest it hurts.

"I'm a higher demon? What does that mean? Why do you think that?"

He turns to me, his gaze shifting over my features slowly in the flickering light.

"You know how many times I've seen the center ring of hell?"

My hair skims against my face as I shake my head slowly at him.

"None. I've never been to this part because it's forbidden. Only hell creatures with immense power would have the ability to ward into here." His features soften and his fingers slide into mine gently. "Come on. We can't linger here. We'll think about your identity crises after we get Professor Zent a souvenir shirt from hell."

I swallow down all the things he just said to me and do my best to push the thoughts from my head. And for the first time in a long time, I just let Phoenix take care of me. I trust him as he guides us deeper into the fiery halls of the underworld.

Until his body goes rigid, and his palm slides over my stomach, halting me in an instant. His finger lifts to his lips, his jade eyes sweeping back and forth over the shadows of the darkness.

That sparkling magic the warlock washed over us is making a hissing sound like it's catching too much heat.

And then the most terrifying thing creeps out of the shadows.

Its small round stature is hip level but there are countless horns curling up from the bald crown of its rigid head. Warts and a charred rough exterior coats his nude body. The bulging mucus colored eyes that fix on me are enough to make the air in my lungs catch with terror.

But the slurred word he whispers over and over is the most terrifying thing of all. It becomes a hissing sound that I can't make out, but it crawls through the hall the closer and closer he gets.

"What—what's he saying, Phoenix?"

Phoenix takes a step back, kicking his shoe against mine.

"*Ass.* He's saying ass. Now run."

Ash flies up all around us, stinging my lungs as we weave down dark corridors with that sound following us every step of the way.

"We need to leave."

"I have to get an item for Professor Zent," I say in a rush.

"We can't. We have to go."

"I'm not failing!" I yell over my shoulder and he irrationally mumbles something about women always taking too long to shop.

"You have three seconds before I tear us away from here. I'm not risking a demonic ass fucking over a goddam gold star from Professor Marty McFly."

He pushes me faster, our feet stumbling as I search the shadows for any little thing I can get my hands on.

"Three," he growls as I frantically search the empty smoky floor.

"Two."

I stop entirely.

His hand grips mine and I look up just in time to come face to disfigured face with the ass troll. Hot air heaves over my cheek with vomit inducing scent clinging to his sticky breath. The pull of interdimensional time tugs at me from the inside out.

It's all slipping away into a darkness.

The flames die out around us.

The heat fades.

It's all nearly gone.

My desperate need to pass is the only explanation I have to for what I'm about to do.

Phoenix's far off voice counts down the very last second just as my palm grips the thing directly in front of me. And I take the only souvenir I have to offer.

The Warlock's Watch sizzles above our heads, just turning to embers when we land directly in front of that big worn desk of Professor Zent's. Dry ash clings to my face, my hair, and even my hand as I slap the item down in front of my Professor with the most triumphant smile tipping my lips.

The thing flops from my hand and rolls a bit, coating the white papers beneath it with a dark red blood that looks severely aged and rotting.

Professor Zent's lips pull down into a heavy frown.

"What—what is that, Miss Izara?" His long finger points at the bloody member, but he doesn't dare touch it.

"That is the cock of an exceedingly rare ass troll, originating from the very center ring of hell. It's quite the collector's item, Professor Zent." My chin lifts high and a humming laughter rumbles out of the soulless man at my side.

"Rare indeed," Professor Zent says, his dull disgust still lingering in his voice. "You've passed with five seconds to spare. Please exit my class and do not return ever again, Miss Izara."

"Thank you," I beam, but the old warlock simply glares at me.

"You are incredibly unwelcome."

TWENTY-FIVE

Izara

The finals drag out through the week.

But today is the day I dread more than any other.

Fucking gym.

Until now, Professor Shade has been infinitely patient with me and my dormant Prod, but when the final comes and we stand grouped with our teams, I notice the sad way his gaze settles on my face. It almost feels like a goodbye. The expression cleaves any confidence I've gained.

"Team one!"

He gestures to the group closest to him and hands their captain a tattered orange flag. The team is lead by the asshole shifter that tried to kill me outside of the gym on that first day. His members are equally massive and brutish and I pray to whatever god or demon is looking out for us that we don't get paired with them.

I should wish less, because the universe just likes to do the opposite of every fucking thing I say.

"You'll be going up against team four." He hands me the thin yellow flag.

I want to cringe away from it, from this whole thing. We never announced a captain, and I'm not captain material. Holding the flag seems like too much responsibility. I turn and promptly shove it into Malek's arms.

Team one's members look at me slowly. Every team has a weak link.

That's me for us.

I am the weakest. And I'm so fucked. So expelled. So thrown into Prod prison where I'll get the death penalty for merely existing...

"Breathe, my heart," Malek's lips skim across my ear lightly. His rasping voice is instantly calming and distracts me from the rising dread inside me.

Phoenix passes the werewolf a death glare for nearly touching me but he thankfully brings his attention back to the task at hand.

"To monitor your progress in this final, I have asked the Headmaster, a few guards, and other professors to help me." Professor Shade's words are a warning to all of us not to break the rules. Not to maim or kill. To control our Prods, to *try* and not do *nothing* at all during this final.

Nothing. The one thing I excel at as a Prod.

After that, the Professor goes to each individual team and separates them into outdoor territories. He tells us where we will start the game and where we are allowed to venture within the woods and academy property. We can only hide our flag within our assigned territory and can only fight our opposing team there as well. Anyone who ventures out is disqualified. Anyone who attacks a team member they weren't pitted against is disqualified.

If anyone fucks up—disqualified.

I don't see myself attacking anyone, honestly. I see myself getting beaten into the dirt, though, so that might be a problem.

"Good luck," Professor Shade says, staring straight at me as though he's sure I'll need it more than most. I probably will, but it's still insulting.

The faerie girl on our team is slow moving when we all start walking. I trail at Syko's side just behind Malek, Saint, and Phoenix. The air is so cold out, I shiver the moment the doors open and we step outside. The skyline is that dark white color that threatens snowfall at any given moment. The three up ahead talk quietly about our opposing team, but they're walking so fast I can barely catch a word they say. This is the last exam, and it's very clear they just want to be done.

I hunch into my thin uniform as we walk and Syko slips his arm loosely around my waist, feeding my body his delicious warmth.

Once we're far enough away from the gymnasium, we all stop and I can't help but shift almost to the very center of them all just to claim as much body heat as possible.

"So," I let out a shaky breath. "What's the plan?" I look from Phoenix to Malek, the smartest of all of us, and I'm surprised to see that none of my teammates seem to care about the final.

Saint's staring up at the pale sky above us like a cat bored out of his mind, his hair sticking up on end, his bright eyes glowing almost manically. Syko looks too tortured to want to take part. He'll give it an effort, I'm sure, I know he's passed every class so far, but he clearly doesn't really care. Phoenix treats this as he's treated every other final. *Effortless.* The bastard doesn't even have to try and he passes with flying colors. It's the same with Malek, but at least he keeps up the pretense that he's anxious with adrenaline. The faerie girl with the resting bitch face stares at her nails, acting like us and this whole situation is beneath her.

"Does no one care about this final?" I dig my nails into my bare arms. We're all freezing our asses off, wearing our gym uniforms, dark blue sweatpants and white shirts with gold and red hems and the academy's insignia on the breast. Comfortable clothes to kick ass in. If I knew *how* to kick ass. There's an endless irony in this whole situation. I *need* to pass this if I want to live. I can't pass this class without a Prod or a team who cares.

Saint smiles, revealing long pointed teeth that gleam in the light. "Should be fun. I don't know about you guys, but that shifter fuck looked like he'd be fun to play with."

He said the word play the same way a psychopath

would say the word 'murder' or 'torture' with unabashed glee.

I think our cat's found a dead mouse to entertain himself with.

"You don't really think we can win against them, do you?" the faerie girl snaps, dropping her hands to her side. She hasn't bothered to tell me her name, and it's been months now, but she has had time to discredit us, it seems.

Her eyes are too bright; an ethereal blue that looks like diamonds on sapphires on diamonds. "Their Prodless is growing into his powers while ours is..." She looks me up and down, pulling her lip back into a vicious sneer. "...pathetic."

My face flames hot. I wish I had a reply to that, but I don't.

She's a gorgeous fae and I'm just some kind of badass demon from a forbidden ring of hell.

I'm epic. Or at least...I will be.

My lips part to tell her just that but Malek beats me to it.

"I think that could work to our advantage." Malek sends me a half smile and an apologetic look. He bends down to the ground and uses his finger to draw a small map of our territory in the light layer of frost that rests against the dirt. He draws the rectangular building that marks Dormitory J and the treeline surrounding it. "I think the best plan is to let Izzy carry the flag."

The only one who protests is faerie girl... and me.

"I can't guard that." It would brand us the losing team before we even begin, not to mention get me killed, expelled, and arrested. Not necessarily in that order. "I'm Prodless."

Malek's smile is reassuring. "Which is precisely why you're the perfect person to guard it, out of all of us. They'll be expecting the strongest of us to be guarding it. They won't expect this."

"Pretty good plan, Scooby," Saint compliments, leaning over to stare at the map. He doesn't bend down, though. It's like he doesn't want to stain his academy provided sweats. How can he look so pretentious in sweats? "But what happens when they realize Phoenix isn't guarding the flag?"

"Who said Phoenix is the strongest?" Malek asks and when all five of us of stare back at him without a word he simply carries on. "We need to separate into three groups. Phoenix and Sasha, you'll stay here." He bends and marks a small X in the middle of the drawn out stick forest.

Her name is Sasha?

When he keeps going I shove the name aside, prepared to forget it already. "It's fortified with trees, and Sasha can make thorns grow around it. Perfect for protecting the flag."

"But *I'm* protecting the flag."

Confusing, sweet, sexy werewolf shifter. His plan makes no sense.

"But the other team won't even consider that a possibility. The goal is to capture the flag. They'll separate into teams, too. They'll come directly to Phoenix and Sasha's location to get it. And they'll have to fight through a tangle of thorns and one pissed off demon just to realize, we're protecting nothing in that spot."

"Ooh, distraction. Very good, Snoopy. You're smarter than you look." Saint disregards the knee stains it will probably leave as he bends low.

Malek ignores his comment and continues, "Izzy, you'll guard the flag, but you'll circle the territory discreetly. They won't expect the flag to be carried by a Prodless so you should be safe."

"*Should be?* They'll fucking tear her apart." It's the first time Phoenix speaks, but I can hear the hard anger and possession in every brittle word. He crouches on the ground bringing his face so close to Malek's it's clearly some game of dominance. "Perhaps you didn't notice, Fido, but the other team's shifter has been looking for an opportunity to rip my feck to pieces. Send her off alone and you'll be sending her to her death."

My feck. It's strange how it almost sounds like he cares.

I let the satisfied feeling wash over me before Saint cuts in, in a voice more serious than I've ever heard from him. "I'll protect her."

Saint? *Saint* who has never offered to work for *anything*, who has never offered to go out of his way for anyone is offering to protect me.

"With my life," he adds. There's a stubborn intensity

about him, a hard set of his lips and eyes as he takes in Phoenix. There's a silent conversation passing between the two, one I don't understand but also can read all too well. It's a promise, a vow.

Phoenix nods.

"So Saint is with Izzy. We need a scout, that's where you come in, Syko." Malek's golden eyes lift to the nephilim, who stands with his arms crossed against his chest. He looks like he hasn't slept in weeks when I know for a fact he barely leaves my bed. It shows in the reflective darkness under his black eyes. "You can fly and scout their positions—discreetly—and come warn us on their location, cause distractions if needed. And I'll capture their flag."

He makes it sound so easy. *Effortless*. I know it will be anything but.

Fireworks shoot off in the sky, raining down over our territory as if the sky itself is bleeding.

"That's the signal." Malek pushes up from the ground. Those of us crouching get up to follow. When I stand, Malek leans in so close the fuming heat of his body burns into me. My whole body trembles as he pushes the hem of my shirt up and tucks the flag into the waistband of my uniform. His fingers linger a bit on the skin on my stomach, like they're addicted to the smooth expanse of flesh. He bends down and his lips skim over mine in the briefest of touches. "Stay safe, *mi corazón*," he commands.

My heart. And, oh, please don't give out on me now, my heart.

It's the first time since that night that he's kissed me. I want to pull him right back to me and memorize the softness of his lips. But we don't have time for fawning over pretty Prods and their pretty words. Not right now.

"Get off my girlfriend," Phoenix grinds out, all but pushing Malek to the side to loom in front of me in his threatening stance. His eyes darken in that demonic way of his that just looks so very hell kissed.

Malek and Phoenix have a hatred between them that goes beyond me.

In a way, I'm the one thing that makes them tolerate each other, I think.

I tilt my chin up even as his body drifts infinitely closer to mine. "Why do you always have to be such a dick?" I chastise him even as I spread my palms against his chest and feel the pure quietness of his heart beneath my fingertips.

His lashes fall to a hooded state as he leans down. The darkness in his eyes spreads like some sort of black river of death. His veins darken and bulge around his eyes. Poison against the skin. A promise of something darker than sex and lust.

"Because the werewolf would completely claim you if I didn't." He's smirking, but I can't tell if he's mocking me or if he's being entirely serious.

His eyes look like darkness and hellfire merged together. It's as terrifying as it is beautiful.

"Stop making out with your boyfriends. We have a game to win," the faerie—Sasha—snaps impatiently.

Phoenix ignores her and bends down so his lips press gently against my own before skimming along the angle of my jaw, to the lobe of my ear. "Stay safe, Feck," he orders vehemently. And then he's pulling away. I hadn't noticed Saint come up behind me, but Phoenix's eyes are there. "With your life, Saint."

I wish I could reply, but he's already walking away.

"He cares about you, he just doesn't realize it yet." Saint turns me around and flashes me his fanged smile. "Now, ready for some fun with flags?"

It's the most happy statement.

Said in the most terrifying way.

I thought a game of capture the flag would be filled with more... excitement than this. So far we're just wandering aimlessly through the woods that borders our dorm. Syko flies up from time to time just to touch back down at my side minutes later. All three of us are tense, and breaking the silence seems forbidden for some reason.

Maybe it's the heavy weight of sadness on Syko's shoulders. He clearly misses Kayos, he's worried about her. I am too. But she's not my sister, and the feeling isn't the same. I want to make him feel better, but I don't have the words.

All of this, it's just a distraction before he's slumped into his thoughts entirely.

Saint lets loose an exaggerated sigh. "This is boring," he complains, stretching his arms over his head in a very feline gesture that shows off the tattoos that shadow his biceps. "We've been walking for twenty minutes and not one person has died yet."

I triple check the yellow flag tucked into the waistband of my uniform. I'm paranoid it'll fall off without me noticing. This game has my nerves scrambled everywhere.

"That's a good thing, though." I pull my shirt back down again and smooth out the wrinkles on the front.

"I'm going to scout." Syko's voice is rough and, a moment later, there's the crunching sound of bones breaking and a whoosh as wings suddenly rip from between his shoulder blades. Blood tinges the tips of the feathers, but they glow golden and fiery, pulsing like blood rushing through the veins. He flaps them once, twice, and then he shoots to the skies. Cold drops of wetness drip onto my cheeks as I watch him go. I swipe my wrist across it and look down to see a smear of blood.

His wings make me curious, and I have so many questions, but don't think it's appropriate to ask him any of them.

"Why did you volunteer to watch over me?" I ask abruptly, wiping the blood on my sweats.

Maybe talking will chase away the nervousness of

this exam. Besides, I'm curious. It's been nagging me since he uttered the words.

Saint, the rich boy who doesn't care about taking notes or passing classes, who has few friends and fewer lovers-Phoenix notwithstanding-offering to look after a nuisance of a feck is just plain odd. Does he have some ulterior motive or is he doing this for Phoenix's benefit and not his own?

Saint taps his fingers against his thigh before he answers. Questions obviously make him hesitant, but I can always tell he answers with honesty in as much of a mischievous way as he can manage. "Why can't I do something from the goodness of my heart without being questioned? It's because I'm a vampire, isn't it? The stereotyping never ends."

My eyes roll so far to the back of my head I'm certain it looks like I'm having a seizure. "Maybe because that goodness of your heart doesn't ever exist unless it benefits you. So cut the shit, Synth Sucker and answer the question."

Banter with him is easy. It's the serious talks that are hard.

Like now.

He flicks his fingers, joining them in odd shapes that look like he's making shadow puppets against his thigh. He's like a junkie desperate for a fix with the constant need to move his hands. I wonder if it's a nervous gesture, something he does to brace himself before he tells the truth.

"That's cold, Feck." He stops moving, shoving his hands into his pockets. "Why wouldn't I help you?"

Because you don't care about anyone but yourself. Because the whole academy is one giant joke to you. Because I'm just a feck you like to tease. Take your pick, I want to scream but bite my tongue against the sarcasm instead.

When I say nothing, he sighs and runs a hand through his silky strands of dark hair. The sun is so low not a ray of light shines across his shadowed face.

"Fine, stop torturing me with your silence, I'll tell you. I'm helping you because I like you. I thought that was obvious. *We're friends.*" He adds that last part like it just occurred to him.

I can't explain why my stomach launches uncomfortably at the word 'friends'. Is that what we are? Is this something I've been unaware of ever since I started fake dating Phoenix? The relationship between me and Saint has been slow building, almost tentative. He's just so hard to read sometimes with all his antagonizing teasing. There are moments when I envy him, his carelessness, and other moments that I know he's as lost as I am. Sometimes, I just want to be lost *with* someone who feels like a disappointment as much as I do.

I enjoy his outlook, though I can't help but wonder if it's a facade he uses to hide what he really feels. And I know the vampire beside me feels deeply. It's in the quiet intensity of his stare when he thinks no one is looking, but I see it. It's bright and colorful and innately *Saint.*

He's like a canvas splattered with paint and I want to peel each layer back bit by vibrant bit.

"Friends," I echo, the word tasting strange on my tongue. "Do friends usually get naked in front of each other and fuck their friend's fake boyfriends?" I don't know why I say that. It doesn't come from a place of jealousy, but from curiosity, and maybe a little envy. They seem close, they *are* close in a way I don't think I can ever be with either of them and I don't know why that hurts so much.

"If it bothers you so much..." I feel the tips of his cold fingers skim up the length of my arm. "... maybe you could join us next time."

A sliver of anticipation slices through my every sense.

Yes, please, I want to beg the words, but nothing comes out except a weak whisper of a sound. A sigh and a whimper roll together to sound fucking pathetic.

"After all," he pulls away and resumes walking in long prowling strides, "what are friends for if not for sharing?"

I want to throw a rock at the back of his stupid head.

I race to catch up with him. "Can you be serious for like two minutes, Saint?"

He guffaws, waving a hand around like he's swatting a fly. "Serious is boring."

"I mean it. Why?"

He stops then and I almost trip over my own feet at the abruptness. We're facing each other now, and he's looking down at me with his intense frost kissed eyes. In them, I can see the secrets he holds like intricate threads in his soul. Pain and anguish, desire, and something else I can't quite place. And I see the truth. A truth he doesn't want to answer, so he avoids it with sarcastic commentary and evasion. But I don't really need the words. Not anymore. Not when I see the answer so clearly in the darkness of the night in the middle of a stupid exam.

Saint Von Hunter is sad. Incredibly, incredibly sad.

And he's not willing to share that truth with anyone. Possibly, not even his best friend.

He turns away from me and keeps walking. He doesn't need to say anything and the intensity of the emotions he locks away is overwhelming. It makes my heart pound and my palms sweat to ignore it.

It makes me feel sick that he's hurting.

We walk a few more minutes before Saint stops me, pressing his palm into my chest. His ears seem to perk like a cat's and he's looking around, sniffing.

He hears something, senses something, it seems.

I peek into the darkness and curse my Prodless eyesight momentarily before the figure he's scenting steps out from the shadows and into the spotlighted illumination of the moon.

She's barefoot with her pale hair in ragged strands. Her night dress is covered in blood and dirt and she's standing preternaturally still.

"Is that..." I take a step forward. *"Kayos?"*

Syko's younger sister cocks her head to the side.

What the fuck is she doing here?

And why does she look like she's been dropped straight out of a horror movie? In the dark I can't tell if the blood is hers or someone else's.

I take a cautious step toward the girl, when all I really want to do is run and pull her into my arms, check if she's okay and call for Syko to come back.

"Are you okay?" My words tremble nervously. "Are you hurt?"

The girl doesn't move.

"Fucking *creeeeeeeeeepy*." Saint tugs at my shirt to pull me back. "Bad idea, Izara. I've seen this in every scary movie ever. Go after her and expect a speedy slasher death to follow."

I shoot him a glare. "What is wrong with you? That's Syko's sister." I try to reach her again but his grip on my shirt is adamant.

"A sister who was arrested and who is a startle Prod. How do you know that's really her? And if it is, I wouldn't let you near her, anyway. Did you happen to miss the bloodstained dorm room she left behind in her wake?"

He has a point.

There are Prods like witches and warlocks at this academy who could easily create a vision like this. How can I be certain this isn't a trick? Still, it looks real enough, she looks real and I can't just stand here next to Saint while she's so close to me, bleeding, and likely traumatized.

"Kayos?" I whisper as if I'm afraid to really say her name out loud.

Bloody Mary. Bloody Mary. Bloody Mary. Circles my mind but I shake the eerie thought away.

The girl takes a tentative step forward like my voice is her beckoning but then she abruptly stops. From here, I can make out the tremble of her jagged nails as she fists them into the tattered nightgown. "I—I'm sorry. I can't," she utters.

"Kayos—"

But then the girl explodes.

I'm propelled backwards by the force of her power. It hits me with a searing pain that rings through my ears, the heat of it scorching down my front. I cry out as I fall. I can hear Saint's painful scream lash out into the night but I can't feel him, can't see him. I can't see anything but the darkness, a shroud placed over my vision. My lungs agonize for air but every gasping pant seems to push me further away from breath rather than closer.

As I fall, my head connects to a rock, and I feel the warmth of blood. Everything else is white noise and confusion. I blink several times and force myself up on my elbows. My vision blurs but I can still see her standing right where she'd been before she erupted. She's shaking, crying in a hysterical crawl of sounds that builds and builds and builds, until it's pressing down on me. And then like magic, she flickers in and out of focus until she's gone completely.

"Saint..." The word slips from my bleeding lips on a

rasp. I force myself up off the ground, even as every muscle shrieks in agony. Even as something seems to stir to life within me. Something *hurts*, it *burns...*

"*Izara.*"

Strong hands grip my arms and haul me up. My vision spots with black dots and it takes me but a few fuzzy moments to realize that the one holding me in his arms, isn't Saint at all.

"Your boyfriend isn't here to protect you now, Feck," the shifter snarls manically just before his head slams into mine and my vision goes black entirely.

TWENTY-SIX

Izara

Stars and white lights dance behind my closed eyelids. The darkness threatens to drown me fully but I force it away.

I have to open my eyes. I don't know what's happening, my brain is muddled with confusion and all I know is that I have to open them.

Bad, bad things happen when I lose consciousness.

Just ask Adam.

"Izara!"

That's Saint's voice.

What happened?

The exam, Syko's sister, the explosion and...

My eyes pry open and I almost regret it as pain ricochets up my skull but I force my eyelids up. Saint is the first thing I see. He's fighting like mad to get to me and my heart nearly splits in half at the sight of three Prods pounding fist after fist into his flesh. He may be a vampire, and he may be strong, but these Prods are savage and outnumber him completely. Fists fly to his face, to his stomach. I hear the crunch of bones, see the flinging of blood, and still he lashes back at them to get to me. He fights like it's the only thing that matters. Like *I'm* the only thing that matters. Even as a Prod grabs his fingers and bends them back at a grotesque angle, it's my name he screams.

"Shut that bloodsucker up," one of them growls.

My skin prickles at that voice. A voice I recognize. The shifter circles around me so Saint is blocked from my vision and I can only see the stranger's massive hulking body.

There's no reply to his command but the sound of Saint's grunts of pain continue.

Hatred flares inside me like a living, breathing thing. It rises up with a sense of familiarity, like a long-lost friend to greet me. I'm sure I've felt this demanding, shaking, adrenaline before.

But where?

It doesn't matter. All that matters is that it consumes me like flames until I'm practically choking on it.

The shifter looms over me. I'm on the ground. I'm weaker, I'm bleeding, my head pounds and blood trails down my temples. I'm nothing compared to him and the vicious claws he sports as he bends to my level. And then his palm is on my face, shoving me into the dirt. He adjusts his grip, flips me, digs his knee into my spine with his hand on my head. The dirt and rocks abrade my cheek.

Pain. All I know is pain and rage and all I want to know is blood and fire.

I feel it crawling up my throat. It's a sensation not quite my own, but inside, buried, now emerging from quiet slumber.

Something rouses in me slowly, unraveling like it's enjoyed its long rest.

But now, it's very much awake.

"Fucking Feck," putrid breath whispers in my ear. "I'm not going to kill you." His voice holds the tone of wicked promise. "But first I am going to hurt you. I'll hurt you so good you'll like it, Feck."

His claws sink into my scalp. I scream then, even if I don't want to give him the satisfaction. Saint responds to my cries with his own. There are thumps of pounding fists and choked words lost in gurgles of blood.

I'm more worried about him than I am for myself. If I wasn't so fucking useless I could help him. I could do something other than lie here and cry.

A fist connects with the side of my face, blinding me briefly with a flash of white across my vision. I gasp.

Anger.

Rage.

A coiling combination of both rises up fully inside of me.

It claws through me with unforgiving hands. I feel it inside and out like an answer to everything I've asked for.

I have the brief sensation of deja vu, of warm phantom hands caressing my cheeks and whispering, *I will protect you now...*

And then something in me snaps right down the middle.

TWENTY-SEVEN

Saint

She's made of stars and fire. It shines in the profound depths of her eyes like the pits of hell and the cosmos beyond heaven itself. She's ephemeral. Iridescent.

And she's fucking beautiful.

The force of her power is the torrent of storms. It's destructive and the impact hurdles towards us like a crashing wave. I fall to my back, the shock ricocheting through my every nerve until I gasp for breath. Bones inside my body crack as quickly as they start to heal and even then it's agony. The pain screams through me entirely but I ignore it as I pull myself up. I think of nothing. Not of the screeching torment of each step or the force of her power ripping through my skin.

I think of nothing but Izara.

The light surrounding her body is blinding, a war of fire and darkness circling her in powerful wisps.

They say the most deadly creatures are often the most alluring.

Her, this woman right now, she could draw the whole world into her lair and consume the poor souls in a single bite. And more would line up in front of her in their absence.

I've never witnessed anything quite like the Prod that rips out of her. She's no feck. She's something else entirely. Something I've never heard of before.

Her arms rise at her sides and she lifts towards the skies like an avenging goddess. Shadows pulsate around her, shooting from her back to form the image of phantasmal wings that flap with powerful strokes. Her palms glow, golden threads of liquid fire flowing through her veins. Her power shoots out from her body like fireworks and the black trees ignite and crumble into ash with a single kiss of her magic.

The entire ground below my feet shakes and splits down the center, It's a jagged line that splinters across the earth and shudders towards Dormitory J. A loud crack pierces the air like raging thunder and the whole dorm shudders just before disaster strikes and the building explodes into showering brick and dust. Debris rains down on me, touching my parted lips as I try to just breathe it all in and understand what's happening around me.

"Izara!" I try to run towards her but my knees shake and give in. I'm still healing, still too fucking weak to get to her. Wind and dust slap against me in one giant wave.

I drag myself across the ground to reach her, my nails cracking as I dig them into the ground to crawl closer to the deadly goddess of a woman. "Izara!"

Rocks strike against my temple, something falls with earth quaking impact. And then after a moment, everything goes still.

I cough and grit my teeth as I stand. My mouth is heavy with ash and the sulfur of deadly magic. My dark lashes lift. Izara slowly drifts down as softly and as gently as the fall of a snowflake. She lands divinely like a heaven-sent angel.

And then her knees give out and she's sprawled on the ground in a matter of seconds.

I can't seem to get to her fast enough.

"Izara?" I slam to my knees and I pull her into my arms, holding her there against me. She's limp and cold to the touch but I can hear the thunderous pumping of her heart, the flowing of her blood, the delicious rapid beating of her pulse.

She's alive.

Jesus Christ, she's *alive*.

Her dark hair is splayed against her skin in sticky strands. I push them away with gentle, trembling fingers.

"Wake up, baby." I cradle her cheek, thumb tracing over the curve. "Please..."

Pain sinks through my quiet chest.

Seeing her like this... it causes something to break inside me. I had one task. One fucking task. To watch her, to protect her with my life and I couldn't do that. I failed her. I failed Phoenix.

I fucking failed myself.

I hold her closer to my chest, her small body feeling fragile against mine.

I couldn't even protect her from herself.

With visceral slowness, her eyes blink open. Beautiful deep brown eyes peer up at me through thick black lashes.

Relief pressurizes my chest as I take in gasp after gasp of air. Her eyelids flutter and I can't help but think she looks like sleeping beauty awakening after the chaos.

Beautiful and tragic.

"Saint..." Her voice is a weak rasp that shivers through me, her expression drawn with confusion. She twists her head to the side just slightly, eyes widening at the sight of the destruction. Her destruction. "What happened?" Her eyes flick back to mine and there's so much fucking trust in her gaze that it damn near cleaves me in two. She shouldn't look at me like that. I don't deserve her trust. I don't deserve her anything.

Why would I, when I couldn't even keep her safe from this?

Fuck.

The aftermath is not going to be good.

I don't want to fucking lose her. It's pathetic how I realize my feelings once everything has gone to shit.

Just as I always do.

"You don't remember?"

She was always so careful with her Prod.

And now I know why.

Her nose scrunches and I'd find the image too damn cute if I wasn't so worried.

"I—I—" her breath shudders past her cracked and bleeding lips.

"She's not a feck. *She's a fucking monster.*" The guttural voice makes me realize that we aren't alone. That the shifters who attacked us broke and healed just like I did. And the one who hurt Izara is looking down at her like she's a beast, like she's a demon.

My earlier rage consumes me all over again. I can feel my fangs lengthening, begging to tear through this fucker's throat.

I extricate myself from Izzy's soft curves slowly and prowl towards the mutt. In barely more than half a blink I'm in front of him, my hand wraps around his throat right over his pulse.

I am going to kill him, drain him of every ounce of his blood.

Fuck the consequences.

"You fucking bastard." I lift his brawny body off the ground, muscles rippling in my biceps. He gasps for breath, claws digging several inches into my arm. His pathetic attempts to fight me off only fuel the beast inside myself.

I've never killed before.

Not fully.

But I'm going to start with him.

And maybe I'll finish with his friends.

Before I can rip out his throat with my fangs, a voice cuts through the haze of my blind rage. "Mr. Von Hunter, please set him down. *Now.*"

Professor Shade suddenly blinks into existence. His eyes barely take in the aftermath of the shit storm around him but I know he's aware. He's glancing at my fingers that are sunk deeply into the shifter's throat and then shifting a watchful look to Izara who stands on shaking knees behind me.

"He hurt her." And he deserves to *die*.

"Let him go."

I can't. Don't want to.

Reckless rage burns through every inch of my body.

But then Izzy's hand's on my arm. Her touch is gentle. Kind. No trace is left of her violent Prod that tore down our dorm, but I know it clings tightly inside her. It's there. And I understand why she hasn't let it out before now.

"Saint."

The broken sound of her voice is the only reason I toss his worthless body near the Professor's feet. The wolf sprawls and scrambles up quickly.

"I didn't do it, Professor!" The fucker looks ready to piss his gym pants as he takes Izara in. Like she's going to kill him with a single look.

Maybe my goddess can.

Izara Castillo is a fucking goddess. And I've never wanted to worship so badly in my life.

The shifter is lucky.

She should have torn him apart. I don't think her conscience could have taken it though. I know she lives in fear of the thing inside her. Of knowing. Of not knowing. Of *hurting*. But fuck, I want him to suffer for what he did to her.

"It was the feck. She—she ripped everything apart."

Izzy's hand on my arm tightens. Her gaze swoops around the destroyed space. The despair is there. Every painful inch of it marrs her beautiful features when she first lays eyes on what she's done.

"I did this?" Her words are barely a weak whisper. Shock tremors through her and I have nothing to offer but the comfort of my hand wrapping around her waist and pulling her close.

"It's alright," I whisper against her temple.

"B—but I couldn't have—I mean—I'm so careful." Panic sets over her. The sentiment is vicious. This whole thing is a clusterfuck. She could get expelled. The raw power inside her... it's too much. Uncontrollable Prods are feared. She can be killed for that alone.

Suddenly, one by one, professors and guards blink into the scene, guided by the Headmaster.

I hate that prick and I barely know him.

He takes one look at the demolished building and sucks in a breath. Izzy clings to me. I won't let her go. Not when this is my fault. If I would have protected her better, none of this shit would have happened.

"Who has done this?" the Headmaster demands, his

gaze closing in on Izzy. She subtly steps back from his watchful gaze, slipping deeper into my arms.

"Headmaster Willms, this Prod attacked his fellow students." Professor Shade shoves the fucking shifter forward.

I watch the wolf and his friends pass. I memorize every single face of the Prods I am going to kill.

"As you're aware, attacking, maiming and killing is against the rules. The four of you broke the rules and therefore are disqualified from the game, have failed the exam, and are hereby placed under arrest." The Professor is cold and unforgiving to the other team in a way I've never seen him be all semester.

The shifter staggers a bit and whirls on the Professor, a look of pure betrayal on his face. "But I—You —You said—"

Professor Shade snaps his fingers with magic stinging the air. The shifter's mouth moves but no words come out, silenced by a form of simple power.

"Take this disgrace of a Prod away." Professor Shade waves a hand toward our attacker.

The guards are immediately there and between one rapid blink of the eye and the next, they're gone, leaving tendrils of smoke in their wake.

Then the Headmaster turns to us.

"And *who* destroyed our school? Confess and perhaps the punishment will be more lenient."

I know better. There's no leniency here. The term

doesn't exist. There's nothing but pain and tears, blood and suffering.

Izara wouldn't survive their punishment. Her deadly Prod wouldn't let her.

She squares her shoulders and steps forward. But I can't bear it. They'll fucking destroy her if I let her go.

I was *supposed* to protect her.

And protect her I will.

"I did it, Headmaster." My voice rings out into the night like a call to the wild.

Headmaster Willms blinks, shakes his head back and forth and stares at me like I've lost my damn mind.

It's never been clearer.

"I don't think I heard you correctly, Mr. Von Hunter. *You* did all of this? A *vampire?*" He motions to the wrecked building behind him.

Wow, talk about bigot. I'm a vampire not a bunny, asshole.

My fingers dig into Izzy's waist in warning before I let my hand drop and step forward. "Yes, Sir. I—I get kind of wound up when I drink too much Type O positive." A smile twists at my lips. Perfect arrogance right in place. It's the look I use when I disappoint my father. With twenty-one years of experience, I've got it down to an art form.

The Headmaster blinks again. "You're a *vampire*." He drags that term through the dirt once more.

My fangs flash. "Kind of you to notice."

I can see the literal confusion swirling around him.

He can't make sense of this. He knows I'm lying, but I'd rather see myself dead and arrested before I let this fuckery of a place harm her.

"How did *you* cause all this destruction?"

My shoulder lifts in a careless shrug. "Homemade bomb. Found a tutorial on the internet, wanted to see if it would work. Looks like it did. The stuff fecks come up with, am I right?"

The Headmaster stutters, beady eyes drifting to Izzy behind me.

Don't look at her, asshole. Look at me.

He clearly doesn't believe me. He has to. He *has* to...

"It's true, Headmaster." Professor Shade steps forward in one form gliding movement. "I was in charge of watching over their section. I saw Mr. Von Hunter detonate it."

"But Miss Castillo—"

"Izara Castillo has shown absolutely *no* promise or hint of powers since she arrived. You really think this feck had anything to do with this?" Professor Shade gestures to the girl he's helped all semester. The *feck*. "Mr. Von Hunter, on the other hand, has done everything he possibly can to get thrown out of this academy."

Yup. That's me.

Finally, someone acknowledges my accomplishments.

I try not to narrow my eyes suspiciously at the Professor though. Why is he helping us? No one ever expects something for nothing. What's his endgame?

The thoughts race through my mind and I have no time to warn Izzy, to question him before the Headmaster declares in a firm voice, "Then, Saint Von Hunter, you are hereby detained for the destruction of the Academy of Six and attacking your fellow classmates."

Wow, he really played judge and jury a little fast there. I wasn't expecting that.

A guard steps towards me with thundering steps and I turn on my heels to face Izara. To see her face one last time because I know what's coming. I know what awaits me.

"Saint, no," she whispers, barely getting the words past her lips.

My hands clasp her own. I relish in the feeling of her warm skin.

"Tell Phoenix I said bye." And because I don't want to spend my life wondering what it would have been like, I press my lips slowly against hers. It's soft, firm, and she gasps against me.

I know I'll remember that sensual sound while I'm rotting away in my cell. I'll remember it even as they push me to madness. I'll remember it even when they sentence me to death.

Her mouth tastes like ash and tears. Hers or mine, I don't know, but I know I'll remember the taste of our goodbye forever.

"Goodbye, Izara Castillo."

"*Don't,*" she whispers on a shaking breath against my

mouth. She makes a move to grab me, to keep me teth-ered to her somehow, but the guard is faster.

A heavy hand clamps on my arm and everything else fades away like sand through a time turner.

I feel no regret as I fall into the void. If I couldn't protect Izzy any other way, then I can do it like this. My final gift to her. If I can't give her anything else, I can give her this.

My life.

My lost soul.

Every single broken piece of me belongs to her now.

TWENTY-EIGHT

Izara

The moment I reach for Saint, my fingers clutch dark smoke instead. It slips through the spaces between my fingers, as empty as the burning holes inside my chest.

He's gone.

And I can't even remember why.

I should fucking *remember* but there are blank spots of nothing where memory should be. If there's one inextricable truth among the chaos, it's that I unleashed my Prod and Saint took the fall for me.

This shouldn't be happening. How many people are going to get hurt because of me, because I can't control what's inside? And *why* can't I remember?

"Get your Prods together," the Headmaster commands in a cold voice. I can barely hear him over the cacophony of my own distressed thoughts.

"Izara?" A hand touches my shoulder. I blink away

tears, I didn't realize I was crying, and find Professor Shade before me. His bicolored eyes are filled with sadness and worry and they flick over me with assessment and curiosity. "Are you alright?"

"He took the fall for me. Why would he do that? Why would he *fucking* do that?" I can feel myself falling apart into thousands of fragmented pieces. My fists slam into Professor Shade's shoulders. My body reacts on a primitive instinct. I pound my anger into him and shout, dissolving into sobs that wrack painfully through my body.

Gentle hands settle against my back.

"Why would you let him lie for me?" I whisper on a gasping voice.

The reality is, I'm the one who should be arrested. I'm the one they should haul off to isolation or prison or whatever terrible fate they have waiting.

And now Saint will die for what I've done.

"What the fuck happened here?" Phoenix's voice slices through me like a fresh wound. It makes me still in the Professor's arms before I take in one shuddering breath and turn to face the demon's wrath.

Black eyes gauge the chaotic mess my Prod created. They flick over every inch of debris and dust before settling on my face, on the blood trickling down my mouth as slow as the dribble of honey that tastes more vile than sweet. Like betrayal and death.

"What happened?" the incubus growls the question, barely concealing the thrum of absolute power radiating from his body, the hatred and the desire for something that surpasses sex. *Vengeance.* "Who did this to you?"

I step forward on shaking knees. I have to be strong, I have to push down the rage that blazes rampantly through my chest, ignore the despair and control the tremors of my voice. "W—we were attacked and..."

His eyes flare like black hellfire, the dark veins around his eyes pulsing. He growls, the sound more demon than human, and whirls around, stomping among broken bits of trees and building.

"Where's Saint?" he demands.

My heart crumbles all over again. Watching Saint get taken had been hard, but this? This is harder. Phoenix and Saint are a unit. Never one without the other. The two are so intricately interwoven into the fabric of each other's lives, I don't want to tell him. But I have to. He has to know.

"They took him, Phoenix. They took Saint." Just saying the words weighs my tongue like there's poison at the back of my throat.

He freezes and turns around slowly to face me. Some hysterical, maddening part of me can't help but admire him in this instant. If I had my paints, I would depict him in his vengeful glory the way he is right now. With his legs apart, standing firm on the rubble of destroyed hopes, hands fisted and white knuckled at his sides, he'd be a picture perfect image of darkness. But it's his eyes I'd have difficulty capturing. I've never seen a rage as powerful as his sudden despair.

The emotion seems so strange, so out of place in the soulless incubus. He claims to feel nothing, but I see it on every sharp line of his beautiful, violent features.

"What do you mean they took him?"he grinds out.

"He—he—" How to explain to him that Saint took the fall for me? That I fucked up on such an astronomical scale that he stepped in to save me? He would despise me for it, and every fragile piece of our relationship that we've spent building would surely crumble along with the remnants of our dorm and Saint's future.

"They arrested him." The Professor steps to my side, pressing a firm hand into my shoulder as if the simple gesture is meant to bring comfort. I'm beyond comfort. All I have is rage and despair, shame and quiet tears. I could easily turn a blank canvas into art, lunch room food into sculptures. I wish I could fucking do something with these emotions inside me.

"*Why?*" The word rips out of Phoenix's throat like a punishment I deserve. Like a whip slicing into flesh. But nothing could ever be more painful than the empty space of the loss of our friend that now lies between us.

"It's my fault." I shake the Professors hold off and step forward as the deadly demon's eyes slice through me. "He was protecting me. I—I'm sorry." My apology is whispered like the weak thing that it is.

The truth is, nothing could ever make up for what I've done.

Phoenix takes a breath, shakes his head back and forth like he's clearing his own muddled thoughts. "It's just confinement, right? He'll be back... Saint will be back..."

The hopeful sound of his voice breaks me a little further.

"The severity of the crime today means he will stand trial with the board of the Academy's directors and the Supernatural government."

"And then?" I ask the Professor, fearing I already know the answer to what comes next.

Bicolored eyes look at me without sadness, but with a firm sort of clarity and, in that moment, I despise him for siding with Saint and lying to cover up what I did. "He will be found guilty and executed for his crimes immediately," Professor Shade says flatly.

"No." Phoenix staggers back, like he can't bear the onslaught of those harsh words. Like everything within him is breaking. Like it took him all this time to realize that something lives inside him, something he can't explain, but it's suddenly tumbling down and breaking him bit by painful bit.

It's love.

The powerful demon falls to his knees, unable to bear the weight of the truth, and digs his fists into the frost-bitten earth. Maybe he'll rip hell up right from the ground and reap it upon our world. Maybe he'll call forth the demons from the pits, sell whatever's left of his tattered soul just to get Saint back.

He'd trade places with Saint in a heartbeat if he could.

But he can't. *We* can't

That knowledge blankets heavily over us, over *him*.

Because when Phoenix next opens his mouth, it's to let out the thunderous roar of dark magic and demonic rage, a force so powerful it shakes beneath our feet and splits the ground anew. I try to go to him, but fall to my hands and knees instead. When the tears come, I just let them fall as I'm filled with the heartbreaking sounds of Phoenix's rage.

And I drown myself in the agony of his screams.

Again.

And again.

And again.

The End.

Thank you for reading Academy of Six. Book two, Control of Five will be available in just three weeks! Get your copy of Control of Five HERE!

ALSO BY A.K. KOONCE

Reverse Harem Books

The Hopeless Series

Hopeless Magic

Hopeless Kingdom

Hopeless Realm

Hopeless Sacrifice

The To Tame a Shifter Series

Taming

Claiming

Maiming

Sustaining

Reigning

The Royal Harem Series

The Hundred Year Curse

The Curse of the Sea

The Legend of the Cursed Princess

The Harem of Misery Series

Pandora's Pain

The Severed Souls Series

Darkness Rising

Darkness Consuming

Darkness Colliding

The Huntress Series

An Assassin's Death

An Assassin's Deception

An Assassin's Destiny

The Villainous Wonderland Series

Into the Madness

Within the Wonder

Under the Lies

The Mortals and Mystics Series

Fate of the Hybrid, Prequel

When Fate Aligns, Book one

When Fate Unravels, Book two

When Fate Prevails, Book three

Resurrection Island

ALSO BY ALEERA ANAY CERES

Reverse Harem Series

Royal Secrets

Secrets Among the Tides

Whispers Beneath the Deep

Caresses Between the Sand

Death Beyond the Waves

The Hybrid Trilogy

Braving the Beasts

Escaping the Beasts

Freeing the Beasts

Royal Lies

Book One COMING SOON!

Anthologies

Hers From the Start

Paranormal Romance Series

Deep Sea Chronicles

Fall in Deep

The Blood Novels

Blood Drug

My Master

Last Hope

Love Bites

Young Adult series

The Last Mermaid

The Witch Games Trilogy

The Witch Games

ABOUT A.K. KOONCE

A.K. Koonce is a USA Today bestselling author. She's mom by day and a fantasy and paranormal romance writer by night. She keeps her fantastical stories in her mind on an endless loop while she tries her best to focus on her actual life and not that of the spectacular, but demanding, fictional characters who always fill her thoughts.

If you want more A.K. Koonce updates, deleted scenes, and giveaways, join her Newsletter or Facebook Reader Group!
AK Koonce Newsletter
AK Koonce Reading Between Realms Facebook Group

ABOUT ALEERA ANAYA CERES

Aleera Anaya Ceres is an Irish-Mexican mix who enjoys reading, writing, art, and heavy fangirling. When she's not dreaming up stories about mermaids, she's daydreaming about all sorts of fantasy creatures. A proud Slytherin from Kansas, she currently lives in Tlaxcala, Mexico with her husband and son.

You can find/contact her here:
Facebook page
Facebook group
Twitter

55440232R00165

Made in the USA
Middletown, DE
16 July 2019